I Want to
Eat Your
Pancreas

I WANT TO EAT YOUR PANCREAS

First published in Japan in 2013 by Futabasha Publishers Ltd., Tokyo.
English version published by Seven Seas Entertainment, LLC.
under license from Futabasha Publishers Ltd.

Seven Seas books may be purchased in bulk for promotional,
educational, or business use. Please contact your local
bookseller or the Macmillan Corporate and Premium Sales
Department at 1-800-221-7945, extension 5442, or by
e-mail at MacmillanSpecialMarkets@macmillan.com.

Follow Seven Seas Entertainment online at
sevenseasentertainment.com.

TRANSLATION: Nathan Collins
ADAPTATION: Nino Cipri
COVER DESIGN: KC Fabellon
INTERIOR LAYOUT & DESIGN: Clay Gardner
PROOFREADER: Kris Swanson, Stephanie Cohen
ASSISTANT EDITOR: Jenn Grunigen
LIGHT NOVEL EDITOR: Nibedita Sen
DIGITAL MANAGER: CK Russell
EDITOR-IN-CHIEF: Adam Arnold
PUBLISHER: Jason DeAngelis

ISBN: 978-1-64275-033-1
Printed in Canada
First Printing: November 2018
10 9 8 7 6 5 4 3 2 1

I Want to Eat Your Pancreas

WRITTEN BY
Yoru Sumino

TRANSLATION BY
Nathan Collins

Seven Seas Entertainment

Table OF Contents

THE DAY OF YAMAUCHI SAKURA'S FUNERAL is dreary and cloudy, entirely at odds with the girl my classmate had been.

I imagine a great many tearful people are at her funeral, their numbers and tears proving her life meant something; but I'm not among them. I didn't attend her wake last night, either. I've stayed home the entire time.

One classmate in particular could have forced me to go, but I guess I'm lucky she can't, since she's no longer in this world. Neither my teachers nor her parents possess the authority or the personal duty to ask me to come. I've been able make my own decision and stick to it.

Seeing as I'm still in high school, I have to go to class whether or not anyone asks me to. But she died during school break, leaving nothing to force me out of the house and into the gloomy weather.

It's morning, and I see both my parents off to work. I scrounge together a lunch before holing up in my room. If you think I'm seeking solitude out of feelings of sadness or the emptiness of loss, you're mistaken.

I've always been the type to stay in my room, unless I had to go to school, or my former classmate dragged me out into the world.

When I'm here, I'm mostly reading books. I don't care for self-help or instructional stuff—novels are my escape of choice. I like to lie in bed with my head on my white pillow and read my books. Hardcovers are too heavy; I prefer pocket-sized paperbacks.

The book I'm reading right now is one I borrowed from her—the only book she treasured, as she was never much of a reader. It's been sitting on my shelf for a while now. I'd intended to read and return it before she died, but I was too late.

I can't change that now. I figure I'll return the book to her family when I'm finished. I'll hold off on paying my respects to her and her family until then.

By the time I finish the book, it's evening. At some point, I closed the curtains and turned on my fluorescent ceiling light so I could still see. My phone rings, and only then do I notice the passage of time.

The call is nothing important; just my mother. I ignore her. She calls a second time, and I ignore her again. The third time, I guess it must have something to do with dinner, so I flip open the phone and put it to my ear. She wants me to get the rice ready before she comes home. I tell her I will and hang up.

Before I return the phone to my desk, I realize something: I haven't so much as touched that device in two days. I don't think I've been purposefully avoiding it, I just haven't thought about picking it up. If that holds some deeper meaning, then I don't know.

I open the flip phone and scroll to the texts, then to the incoming folder. Zero unread messages. That's hardly a surprise. Next, I look at the sent folder. Aside from calls, I see evidence of the last time I used the device.

A text message I sent to the girl who had been my classmate.

Just one sentence.

I don't know if she ever saw it.

I consider going to the kitchen but instead flop back into bed. All I can think about is what I wrote to her.

Did she ever see my message?

I want to eat your pancreas.

If she did see it, how did she take it?

I fall asleep, still trying to find an answer.

The rice doesn't get made until my mom comes home.

I'm not sure, but I think I meet the girl in my dreams.

One

"**I** WANT TO EAT YOUR PANCREAS," she said.

Yamauchi Sakura's bizarre non sequitur came as I was dutifully organizing the books in the school library's dusty stacks, as was my responsibility as a librarian's assistant.

I considered ignoring it, but she and I were the only people there, and the remark was clearly intended to inspire morbid curiosity. That meant she was talking to me.

Having no other choice, I responded without turning around. If she was doing her work, her back would still be to me.

"What," I said, "did you suddenly realize you're a cannibal?"

She took a deep breath, coughed a little from the dust, then explained with some pride, "I saw this story on TV last night. In old times, when something was wrong with someone's body, they would eat that part of some animal."

I kept on not looking. "And?"

"If their liver was bad, they'd eat liver; if their stomach was bad, they'd eat stomach. I guess they believed it would heal them. So, I want to eat your pancreas."

"My pancreas?"

"I don't see anyone else's pancreas here."

She giggled. I heard the sound of hardcover books being rearranged on a shelf; so she was still working and hadn't stopped to look my way.

I said, "I'd rather you not hang all the pressure of saving your life on one tiny organ in my body."

"You're right. All that stress might take out your stomach, too."

"Go lay this on someone else, then."

"Like who? I can't say I like the idea of eating my own family."

She giggled again. I didn't; I was taking my job seriously. I wished she would learn from my example.

She continued, "That's why you're the only one I can ask, [Classmate Who Knows My Secret]-kun."

"And in this scenario you're imagining, you don't suppose that I might need my pancreas for myself?"

"You don't even know what a pancreas does," she teased.

"Sure I do."

I did know. I hadn't always known, of course—I'd needed to look it up. I wouldn't have had any reason to if not for her.

This made her happy, and she turned toward me. I could tell both from the sound of her breathing and the movement of her feet. Turning only my head, I gave her a quick glance. Her expression was so happy, her face alive with beads of perspiration. It was hard to believe she would be dead soon.

She wasn't the only one sweating. It was July, with global warming in full effect, and the air conditioning struggled to extend to the archive room.

Gleefully she said, "Don't tell me you looked it up."

I might have tried to avoid answering, but she was too worked up to let this go. Better to just get it over with.

"The pancreas regulates digestion and metabolism," I said. "For instance, it secretes insulin that converts sugar into usable energy. Without the pancreas, people can't make energy, and they die. I'm sorry, but I can't offer you mine on a platter."

As I turned my attention back to my work, she howled with laughter. I figured my tiny quip must have gone over better than I'd expected, but that wasn't why she laughed.

"How about that," she said. "You've taken an interest in me after all, haven't you?"

I took a moment to form an answer, then said, "A classmate dying of a serious illness is always going to be interesting."

"No, I mean *me*, as a person."

I paused. "Who can say?"

"Oh, come on!" she said with more laughter. The heat must have dazed her, making her not think straight. I worried for her condition.

I kept working in silence until the librarian came to get us.

It was time to close up the school library for the day. I slid a book partly off the shelf to mark my position, then looked around to make sure I hadn't forgotten any of my possessions. We exited the sweltering archives for the library's main room, where the cool air struck my sweaty skin and sent a shiver down my body.

"It feels so nice in here," my classmate said, as she twirled her way behind the circulation desk. She retrieved a towel from her school bag and wiped her face. I followed her—at a slower pace, and without the spinning—and dried myself off, too.

"Good work today," the forty-something female librarian said. "You can stay and relax a bit if you'd like. Here, I prepared some tea and sweets."

"Wow!" the girl said. "Thanks!"

"Thank you," I said.

I took a drink of the cold barley tea and gazed across the library. All the other students had left.

My classmate bit into a sweet bun and said, "This manjuu is delicious."

She had a habit of reacting to every single positive thing around her.

She had already claimed a chair behind the counter. I took a pastry for myself and moved the other chair a little farther from her before sitting on it.

"Sorry to take you away from your study time," the librarian said. "I know exams are next week."

"Don't worry about it," the girl said. "We always do fine— right in the middle of the pack. Isn't that right, [Classmate Who Knows My Secret]-kun?"

"Sure," I said noncommittally, "as long as I listen in class, I do all right." I bit into the manjuu. It really was delicious.

The librarian asked, "Have you thought about what you're doing for college, Yamauchi-san?"

"Not yet," she replied. "Or maybe I don't feel like I need to."

"And you, [Well-Mannered Student]-kun?"

"I haven't either," I said.

Reaching for a second manjuu, the girl protested, "You can't be that way, [Classmate Who Knows My Secret]-kun. You have to think about the future."

I ignored her meddling and drank another sip of tea. The store-bought drink tasted good, and familiar.

The librarian said, "You both have to think about your futures. If you don't pay attention, you'll be as old as I am before you know it."

The girl gave me a glance, then laughed pleasantly and said, "Aw, that won't happen." The two exchanged a chuckle, but not me. I took another bite of my pastry and washed it down with the barley tea.

My classmate was right. It wouldn't happen.

She would never be as old as the librarian, and only she and I knew it. She had only glanced at me, but I found it about as subtle as a stage wink from some Hollywood actress telling a joke.

Just to be clear, the reason I didn't laugh wasn't because her joke was too risky. Rather, I was irritated by her self-satisfied, *Look at me, I'm saying something funny* expression.

She returned my sullen lack of reaction with a sharp, frustrated glare, and she kept it on me until I finally offered her a slight upturn of a smile.

We sat in the closed library for about a half an hour before deciding to go home.

It was just past six in the evening when we reached the shoe cubbies inside the school's entrance, but the sun was still going strong. Through the open doorway came the energetic voices of student athletes practicing after school sports.

"It sure was hot inside there today," the girl said.

"Yeah," I replied.

"I hope it's not that bad tomorrow. At least after that, it'll be the weekend."

"Yeah," I replied.

"Are you listening to me?" she asked.

"I'm listening."

I exchanged my indoor school slippers for my outdoor shoes and went outside. In front of the building's main entrance was a small courtyard and the front gate, with the sports grounds on the opposite side of the school. As I walked, the voices of the baseball and rugby players gradually dimmed.

Stomping her feet, my classmate caught up to me and demanded, "Didn't anyone ever teach you to listen when other people are talking?"

"Sure they did. I said I was listening."

"All right then, so what was I talking about?"

I thought a moment, then said, "The manjuu."

With the cheerful chiding of a daycare teacher, she said, "You weren't listening! You mustn't tell lies."

I was short for a boy my age, and she was tall for a girl, which left us at about the same height. There was something refreshing about being scolded by someone just a little bit shorter than me.

"Sorry," I said, "I was thinking about something."

"Oh?"

Her frown disappeared as if it had never been there and she leaned in, peering at me with intense interest. I briefly hastened my pace to regain a little distance, then I bobbed my head and said, "Yeah, it's something I've been thinking about for a while. Seriously, too, for once."

"Whoa! Well, out with it."

"I've been thinking about you."

I was careful not to turn this into a dramatic scene. I didn't stop walking, I didn't look at her; I tried to say it as casually as I could. I knew if she took what I said too seriously, she would be a pain about it.

But being a pain was who she was, and her reaction trampled all over my careful maneuvering.

"About me?" she gasped. "Is this what I think it is? Are you about to confess your love to me? You're getting me all flustered!"

I waited until she was finished. Then I said, "Not like that."

"I'm listening."

Still keeping my tone utterly casual, I asked, "Is it really all right for you to be spending what little time you have organizing books in the school library?"

She tilted her head in confusion. "Well, yeah, obviously. Why wouldn't it be?"

"I don't think there's anything obvious about it."

"Oh?" she asked. "And what do you suggest I should be doing instead?"

"Don't you have a lot of things you want to do? Like meeting up with your first crush, or maybe hitchhiking around in foreign countries until you find the place you want to spend your last days?"

This time she tilted her head in the opposite direction. She hummed in disagreement and said, "I get what you're saying, but... Let me put it this way: you have things you want to do before you die, too, right?"

"I guess so."

"Yet you're not doing them. Either one of us could die tomorrow. That goes the same for you and just as much for me. Every day is worth the same as any other. What I did or didn't do today doesn't change its worth. Today, I had fun."

I thought it over for a moment, then said, "Okay."

She had a point. As much as I didn't want to agree, I found myself seeing the truth in it.

Just as she would die one day soon, so, too, would I. I couldn't know when, but it was certain. It was entirely possible I might die before she did.

Having to face her own mortality had given her remarkable insight. Just a bit, I reassessed my opinion of the girl walking beside me.

Not that she would care how I estimated her. She was liked by far too many people for her to bother over how someone like me felt.

Just then, a boy in a soccer uniform came running from the direction of the front gate. The moment he saw her, his expression brightened.

Sakura noticed him and gave him a small wave, saying, "Go get 'em!"

"See you, Sakura," he said.

He jogged past us with a breezy smile and an easy, confident step. He was in our class, but he didn't even give me a glance.

"That jerk," the girl said. "He ignored you, [Classmate Who Knows My Secret]-kun. I'll have to teach him some manners tomorrow!"

"You don't have to. Actually, please don't. It doesn't bother me."

It really didn't. Of course, our classmates would treat us differently—she and I were about as opposite as two people could be. Nothing would change that.

"That attitude is why you don't make any friends," she said.

"It's just the truth. Don't waste your time."

"See," she groaned, "that's exactly what I'm talking about."

We'd reached the school's front gate. My house and hers were in opposite directions, and this was where we always parted. I wished we didn't have to.

"Later," I said. I wasn't going to show my regret now.

I was about to turn away from her when she stopped me by saying, "Listen. About what you said..."

She had a pleased look on her face, with an impish smile that meant she had probably just thought of some way to mess with me. Whatever my face looked like, I was sure it wasn't pleased.

"I suppose," she said, "that if you're so insistent about help-ing me spend what little time I have left more wisely, I could let you."

"What do you mean?"

"Are you doing anything Sunday?"

"Sorry," I said. "I have a date with this girl. She's really cute, but if I don't spend time with her, she gets all hysterical and it turns into this big whole thing."

"You're lying, aren't you?"

"What if I am?"

"Then it's settled," she said. "Meet me in front of the train station at eleven on Sunday morning. I'll write about it in my memoir, so you'd better come."

Showing no actual concern or need for my assent, she waved goodbye and began walking home. Beyond her, the summer sky gazed down upon us, with its orange and pink only just starting to give way to ultramarine.

Without waving, I turned my back to her and started walk-ing. As I took the familiar way home, the boisterous chatter and laughter around the school faded away, and the deep blue gradu-ally claimed the rest of the sky. I saw the same streets I always did, and she saw the same streets she always did, but I got the feeling how we saw them was completely different.

I would keep walking this same path until I graduated high school.

I wondered how many more times she would walk hers.

Then I remembered what she said. I couldn't know exactly

how many more times I would walk mine. I shouldn't see my path any differently than she saw hers.

I held a finger to my neck to make sure I was still alive. I took a step with each pulse of my heartbeat, and my mood soured by the forced awareness of the transience and fragility of my life.

A cool evening breeze came along and distracted me from this train of thought. I decided to think of something more positive—deciding whether or not I would leave the house on Sunday.

Two

IT HAD STARTED IN APRIL, when the late-blooming sakura trees still held their cherry blossoms.

Medical science continued to make advancements, whether I knew about them or not, and I mostly didn't. Nor did I care to.

What I later learned was that modern medicine had advanced far enough to permit at least one girl a normal life, even when a serious illness left her with less than one year to live. So normal was her life that if she chose to keep her disease a secret, no one would suspect a thing. In other words, mankind had gained the power to extend her life as it was before.

When I thought about it, carrying on as if everything was normal—despite suffering a serious illness—seemed more machinelike than human. But no one in that position had any reason to give a damn about what I thought.

My classmate certainly didn't let any such concerns obstruct her from enjoying the benefits of modern medical science.

She'd been sloppy letting her secret out, and unluckily it was to someone like me—just some guy who happened to be in the same class as her.

The day I'd learned her secret, I went to the hospital instead of school for my appendectomy—not the surgery itself, but because I needed to get the stitches taken out. The doctor said I had recovered fine, and the stitch removal was over quickly. I would have been able to go back to school, if only just a little late, but the wait had been long, typical of a large hospital, and I was inclined to take the excuse to skip. And so, I lingered in the lobby for a while.

The events that followed were caused by a mere passing impulse. I noticed a book stranded on a solitary couch in the lobby's corner, some distance removed from the other seating. I assumed someone must have accidently left the book behind. Curiosity and anticipation filled me, of the kind only a bibliophile knew, and the impulse compelled me into motion.

I weaved my way through the waiting patients to the couch and sat there. The paperback-sized book was fairly thick; at first glance I judged it to be at least three hundred pages. Its owner had added a protective cover, made of paper, that I recognized from a bookstore near the hospital.

I removed the outer cover and was a little surprised by what I found. Instead of an actual dust jacket, someone had handwritten on the blank cover with a thick magic marker: *Living with Dying.* The name didn't ring any bells, either as the title of a book or a potential publisher.

Since thinking about it couldn't make me remember something I didn't know, I flipped the book open to the first page. The words weren't printed in a familiar typeface, but rather written neatly in ballpoint pen.

Someone had written this by hand.

November 23—

Starting today, I plan to record my thoughts and activities in this book, which I'm titling "Living with Dying." I'm not telling anyone outside my immediate family, but in a few years, I'll be dead. I'm writing this so I can accept it, and so I can keep on living with my sickness. As for what's wrong with my pancreas, so far, it's all mostly been over my head. They say the disease was only isolated and identified recently. At the time, everyone who had it died almost right away, but now the doctors can keep most of the symptoms from showing.

My eyes stopped taking in the words as I tried to process what I'd read. A few words, things I'd never had cause to say aloud before, escaped my lips unbidden.

"Pancreas... I'll be dead."

It was a diary, chronicling someone's battle with—or rather, co-existence with—a terminal disease. This wasn't something I should read.

I was closing the journal when someone spoke to me.

"Um..." she said.

I looked up and saw a girl from my class. I was surprised because I knew who she was, but I didn't let it show on my face. She may have approached me for some reason unrelated to the book.

Usually, not much bothers me, but looking back, I think that part of me didn't want to accept the possibility one of my peers had been doomed to an imminent death.

I put on the sort of mildly interested expression that you give a classmate who comes over to talk to you and waited for her to say something. She held out her hand, palm up, and made a mockery of my flimsy hopes.

"That's mine," she said. "How come you're at the hospital, [Unremarkable Classmate]-kun?"

I'd barely exchanged a few words with her before this moment, and I knew nothing about her except she was cheerful and bubbly, completely unlike me. I was taken aback; someone she barely knew had come into knowledge of her serious illness. How, then, could she wear such a brave smile?

I decided to pretend I hadn't read any of it. It would be for the best—both for me and her.

"I had my appendix removed last week," I said. "I had to get the stitches taken out."

"Oh, I see. They had to run some tests on my pancreas. If the doctors don't keep an eye on it, I'll die."

What was she doing? I was trying to be considerate, and she was shattering my efforts. I tried, unsuccessfully, to read her expression and figure out her true intentions. Her smile deepened, and she flopped onto the couch next to me.

"Is that such a surprise?" she asked. Then, as casually as if she were recommending any normal novel, she said, "You started reading it, didn't you—*Living with Dying?*"

I thought, *So that's what this is—just some practical joke.* It just happened to be me who took the bait. That we were passing acquaintances was just coincidence.

"All right, I'll come clean," she started saying. This was it. Time to reveal the joke. "You caught me by surprise. When I realized my book was missing, I came here frantically searching for it, and I find you holding it."

She was losing me. "What's this all about?"

"My book. *Living with Dying.* You were reading it. I started writing in it, kind of like a journal, after I found out about my pancreas."

"This is a joke, right?"

She let out a roaring laugh, undeterred by the hushed hospital setting. "Just how dark a sense of humor do you think I have? Some twisted prank that would be. No, what I wrote is real. My pancreas doesn't work, and I'm going to die soon. That's what it is."

I paused for a beat that stretched on to something longer.

"Oh, okay," I said.

"What?" she said, sounding disappointed. "That's all you have to say?"

"Well, what's someone supposed to say when they find out their classmate is going to die soon?"

She hummed in thought. "I'd probably be too stunned to say anything."

"Right. Really, you should be impressed I managed to say any-thing at all."

"Good point," she said with a giggle. I didn't see what she found so funny.

With that, she took back her book and waved goodbye. Before leaving for the examination rooms, she said, "I'm keeping it a secret from everybody, so don't tell anyone in class, okay?"

After she left, I mostly felt relief, confident this would be the end of our interaction.

But then the next morning, she came up to me in the hallway to say hi. And then, worse yet, she volunteered to join the student librarians—rather, student *librarian,* I should say, as the students in our school were free to decide our own activities, and up un-til now, I was the only one who'd chosen to work in the library. I didn't understand what reason she had to join me, but I'd always been the type to just go where the flow took me, and I didn't put up a fight. Dutifully, I taught the new librarian how to do our work.

Arguably, it was that single paperback journal that led me to stand outside the train station at eleven on Sunday morning. You never can know what will act as a trigger.

I was like a boat made of reeds, flowing with life's currents, never one to turn against a strong force. So I didn't reject her in-vitation—not that she gave me an opening to reject it—and here I was at the meeting place.

I supposed I could have stood her up, but if I wronged her, it would have only given her something to hold over me, and who knew what she would demand of me then. Unlike me, she was an icebreaker ship steering whichever way she pleased. To oppose her head-on would be unwise.

The sculpture in front of the station was a popular meeting place in our town. I arrived there five minutes early; she showed up right on time.

I hadn't seen her dressed in anything but the school uniform since our encounter at the hospital. She was wearing a simple outfit of a T-shirt and jeans.

She walked over with a grin, and I half-raised my arm in greeting.

"Morning!" she said. "I was just wondering what I'd do if you stood me up."

"I'd be lying if I said I hadn't considered it," I admitted.

"But it looks like it worked out."

"I'm not sure that's quite how I'd phrase it, but sure. So then, what are we doing today?"

"That's the spirit. Now you're *gettin' into it.*"

The sun was bright, and she wore that same grin that seemed to make her true situation a lie. Incidentally, I wasn't, quote, gettin' into it.

She said, "Let's go to the city and figure it out from there."

"I don't like crowds," I replied.

"Do you have enough money for the train? I can give you some if you need."

"I've got enough."

She easily plowed through my meager resistance, and we were soon on our way to the city. As I'd feared, the massive train station, with its variety of shops and restaurants, was packed with enough people to overwhelm anyone who was uncomfortable around strangers.

Walking beside me, my classmate was in perfectly fine spirits, seemingly unphased by the volume of people around us. I again found myself doubting that she would soon be dead, even though she'd presented me with plenty of official papers that left no room for doubts.

We exited the turnstiles, and though the crowds grew thicker, she pressed on without hesitation. Then—finally—she told me what we had come for.

"First up—yakiniku!" she exclaimed.

"Yakiniku? It's still morning. I hardly feel like grilling a bunch of meat this early in the day."

"Does meat taste any different in the afternoon or at night?"

"I can't say I've personally noticed a difference, but then again, I don't eat meat all day."

"Then there's no problem," she said. "I want to eat yakiniku."

"I had breakfast at ten," I said.

"It'll be fine. Everyone likes yakiniku."

"Don't you want to at least discuss it?"

Apparently, she didn't.

All further protests were in vain. The next thing I knew, I was seated across the table from her, with the standard tabletop charcoal grill between us. I had the boat of reeds act down pat. The lighting was low, but we could see each other just fine—even if we didn't really need to—thanks to the pendant lights above each of the mostly empty tables.

Before long, a young waiter crouched at the end of our table to take our order. I wasn't sure what I was supposed to do, but my classmate easily responded like a math student reciting a well-memorized formula.

"We'll take this course," she said, pointing at the menu. "The most expensive one."

"Hold up," I interjected. "I don't have that much money on me."

"It's fine. I'm paying." Then to the waiter, she continued, "The most expensive all-you-can-eat course." She glanced at me. "Oolong tea should be fine for our drinks, right?"

Caught up in her momentum, I nodded. The waiter hurriedly repeated the order and ducked back into the kitchen. Maybe he was worried my classmate might change her mind.

Gleefully, the girl said, "Oh, I'm looking forward to this."

"Um," I said, "I'll pay you back later."

"I said it's fine. Don't worry about it. It's my treat. I have some money saved up from my after-school job that I have to burn through."

Before I die, she didn't say, but I was sure that was what she meant.

"This is even worse than your decision to join me at the library," I said. "I'm telling you, you've got to spend your time on something more meaningful."

"This *is* meaningful. It would be no fun eating yakiniku all by myself, now would it? I'm spending my money for my enjoyment."

"Yeah, but—"

Just as I was mounting my resistance, the waiter reappeared, saying, "Two oolong teas. Sorry for the wait."

The girl had on a big grin. She couldn't have orchestrated a better way to escape an unwelcome topic.

After the tea came a plate piled high with meat. The various artfully arranged, thinly sliced cuts looked expensive and delicious. Marbled, even. It almost looked good enough to eat raw, though that would have likely drawn some complaints.

The wire mesh grill seemed to have heated up enough, and the girl excitedly put on her first slice of meat. The pleasant sizzle and aroma socked me straight in the stomach. I was, after all, still a growing boy, and fighting hunger wasn't a winning battle. I chose a cut of meat and placed it on the grill next to hers. The high-quality beef cooked quickly above the hot coals.

"Itadakimasu!" she said, offering a quick word of thanks to whoever was listening. She retrieved her meat with her chopsticks and ate it with a "Yum!"

"Itadakimasu." I ate mine and remarked, "Okay, it's pretty good."

"What?" she said. "That's all your reaction is? It's freaking delicious, right? Or am I just making more out of this because I'm dying soon?"

No, it really was delicious. I just wasn't as keyed up about it as she was.

As we kept eating, she said, "This is so good. This must be how rich people eat all the time."

"I don't think rich people go to all-you-can-eat places."

"That's too bad for them. They could be eating all this tasty meat all they want."

"Everything's all-you-can-eat to a rich person," I said.

I hadn't thought I was especially hungry, but soon our plate for two was empty. She picked up the menu from the edge of the table and looked it over.

She asked, "Are you all right with whatever?"

"I'll leave it to you," I said.

I'll leave it to you. That phrase suited me well.

Without a word, she raised her hand, and the waiter appeared fast enough to make me suspect he'd been watching us. I shrank back a little, feeling put off by his excessive devotion to his job. My classmate glanced at me over the menu as she rattled off her order.

"Reed tripe, baby bag, rifle, bee's nest, raincoat, heart, necktie, heart stem, airbags, book tripe, and sweetbread."

"Wait a minute, wait a minute," I said. "What on earth are you ordering?"

I felt awkward getting in the way of our waiter's job, but I couldn't help cutting in when my classmate was saying all these unfamiliar things.

"Necktie?" I asked. "Like the kind you wear?"

"What are you talking about?" she said to me. Then to the waiter, she added, "Don't mind him. Just bring out one order of each cut."

The waiter nodded, then left to put in the order with a pleasant smile.

I was still trying to catch up. "You said something about bees. Do they serve bugs here?"

"Don't you know?" she said. "Necktie and bee's nest are words for certain parts of a cow. I like eating offal."

"You mean like cow organs? I didn't know cow parts had such unusual names."

"Not just cows—we do too, you know. Like the funny bone."

"I guess."

"And by the way, sweetbread is the pancreas," she said.

I asked, "You're not eating cow organs to try to heal yourself, are you?"

"I just think they taste good. If someone asked me my favorite thing, I'd answer offal. I love it!"

"I'm not sure what to say to that."

"I forgot to order rice. Do you need any?"

"I don't," I said.

After a little while, the server returned with a large platter almost overflowing with beef organs. The picture was even more grotesque than I'd imagined, and I immediately lost my appetite.

My classmate ordered some steamed rice and began happily placing pieces of meat onto the grill. I helped her out of obligation.

She looked at me, noticing I wasn't helping myself to the oddly shaped cuts. "Here, this one's done," she said, placing a whitish mass with a honeycomb-like pattern onto my plate. Since

I didn't believe in letting food go to waste, I pushed through my trepidation and put it into my mouth.

"Tastes good, right?" she said.

Truth be told, it was much better than I expected. The meat was savory and had a pleasant texture. But I was beginning to feel vaguely annoyed, like she was having fun at my expense, and I decided to answer with a vague shrug. She grinned at me, though I didn't understand why; I rarely did.

I noticed she was out of tea, so I called over the waiter and ordered her a refill along with some normal meat.

I mostly ate the regular meat, and she mostly munched on the offal. Sometimes I would eat a piece of the organs, and she'd give me that irritating grin. But then I stole another piece from her just as she'd finished carefully cooking it, and her yelp of protest made me feel a little better.

We were having a good time, when suddenly she said, "I don't want to be cremated."

It was so out of place, all I could respond with was, "Huh?"

I thought I might have heard her wrong, but her expression turned serious. She repeated, "I don't want to be cremated. After I die."

"We're grilling meat, and that's seriously what you want to talk about?"

She went on. "It's like permanently removing someone from the world. I wonder if I could just have everyone eat me instead."

"Let's not talk about your dead body while I'm trying to have some meat, okay?"

"You can eat my pancreas," she said.

"Hello," I protested. "Are you listening to me?"

"I've heard some cultures believe that, when you eat another person, their soul goes on living inside you."

I was right, she wasn't listening. Either that, or she was choosing to ignore me. The latter seemed more likely.

"Do you think people would do that for me?" she asked.

"No, I'm pretty sure that won't be possible. Ethically, at least. I couldn't say if it's legal or not without looking up the laws."

"That's too bad," she said, sounding sorry for me. "Now I won't be able to give you my pancreas."

"I don't need it."

"Maybe you don't *need* to eat it, but don't you want to?"

"Your pancreas is what's going to make you die, right? If your soul is going anywhere in your body, that's definitely where it's ending up. And your soul sounds like too much of a troublemaker for me—it would just be a constant racket."

"I'd believe it," she said with a hearty laugh.

If she was this noisy alive, then her pancreas, once imbued with her spiritual essence, would certainly be too. No, thank you.

If she knew any restraint, she didn't show it. Between the meat, rice, and organs, she ate so much more than me, to the point of groaning in pain. Meanwhile, I stopped once I felt pleasantly stuffed. The first order had been enough for me, and unlike her, I hadn't foolishly packed the table with side orders.

After we finished, the waiter took away our pile of empty plates and the spent grill, then returned with sherbet for dessert.

Despite all her moaning about feeling sick and being in pain, the icy treat spurred her back to life. She took a deep, reinvigorated breath, and she was back to making that racket again.

I asked, "Don't you have any dietary restrictions?"

"Not really. But that's only thanks to the last ten years of medical advancements. It's amazing what people are capable of achieving. I'm sick, but it doesn't get in the way of my life at all—even though sometimes I wish they'd focus all that effort on a cure instead."

"Yeah," I said.

I didn't know anything about medicine, but for once I saw no harm in agreeing with her. I'd heard something about how medical science was focused on helping people live with terminal illnesses, rather than curing them instead. The way I saw it, research should have focused on curing diseases rather than accepting them. Not that my opinion would cause any progress to be made. No, if I wanted anything to change, I would have to go through specialized studies and become a medical scientist first. She didn't have that kind of time, and I didn't have the inclination.

"What's next?" I asked.

"Like, in my future?" she asked. "I don't have one, remember."

"That's not what I meant. You know, I've been meaning to say something—when you joke like that, don't you see how it puts me in a bad place?"

She looked at me with confusion, then giggled a little. Her expression could totally change in an instant. It was hard to believe she was the same species as me. That would at least explain the shorter lifespan.

She said, "You're the only person I can talk like that with. Most people would shy away from me. But not you—you're amazing. You can talk with a dying classmate just like everything was normal. I don't think I could do that. You're special. When I'm with you, I can say whatever I want."

"I'm not that special," I said. I didn't think I was at all.

"Well, agree to disagree. You know, I've never seen you looking sad around me. Could it be that you cry for me when you're at home?"

"I don't."

"You should."

I wasn't about to. That wasn't for me to do. I didn't feel sad, and even if I did, I wasn't about to reveal it in front of her. She shouldn't expect other people to grieve when she wasn't showing any misery herself.

"Back to my question," I said. "What's next? This afternoon."

"You changed the subject! So you *do* cry for me. I'm going to go buy some rope."

"I don't cry for you. And what do you mean, rope?"

"I see, you're putting up a tough front to win over my feminine heart. You heard me, rope. Like for hanging yourself with."

"Who would bother trying to win over someone who's about to die? And are you planning on killing yourself?"

"I don't know. I was thinking about it. Better to do it myself than let the illness kill me. But I'm not thinking about doing it yet. The rope is just for a practical joke. And hey, you shouldn't say such mean things to me! What if you hurt my feelings and drove me to suicide?"

"A practical joke?" I asked. "Listen, I think our conversation is getting all mixed up. Can we just talk about one thing at a time?"

"Sure," she said. "Have you ever had a girlfriend?"

"I'm not even going to ask how you landed on that subject, and you don't have to tell me."

She looked like she was about to say something, and I stood up before she could. Not seeing our check on the table, I called over the waiter who instructed us to pay up front.

"I guess we're going then," my classmate said, grinning.

It appeared she could be moved on from a conversation if I didn't take her bait. Finally, something I could use to my advantage. I made a mental note to use that tactic again.

Full-bellied, we left the yakiniku restaurant and went above ground, where the bright summer sun glared down at us. Reflexively, I squinted.

"What a beautiful day," she said, just softly enough that I wasn't sure if I was meant to respond. "Maybe I should die on a day like this."

I decided to stick with my newfound strategy: ignoring her, like how people say not to look a wild animal in the eyes.

We started walking toward a large shopping mall directly attached to the train station. On the way, we shared light conversation, although if you guessed she did most of the talking, you'd be right.

A home improvement center anchored the mall. Nobody sold ropes specifically for hanging oneself, but they'd probably have something close.

The mall was packed with bustling crowds, but the store's rope aisle was empty. The only people looking to buy rope on a nice day like this were probably contractors, cowboys, and dying schoolgirls.

I went a little farther down the aisle to compare nail sizes. I could hear some children laughing and playing somewhere in the store. I also heard my classmate call over a young worker and say to him, "Excuse me, I'm looking for a rope to hang myself with. Now, I don't want to leave any marks on my skin, so I was wondering which rope is the safest for that."

I turned to look, and the employee's expression was so bewildered it made me laugh a little. Then I felt annoyed at the girl for making another of her jokes at my and the worker's expense. A safe suicide—that was just the kind of idea she'd find funny. And now she had me laughing, too. Without bothering to make sure I put the correctly sized nails into their proper containers, I replaced them and approached the put-upon worker. My classmate's back was to me, but from the way she was moving, I could tell she was giggling.

"I'm sorry," I said, offering him rescue. "This one doesn't have much time to live. She's a little touched in the head."

I couldn't tell if he'd accepted my story or if he'd just gotten disgusted with us, but either way, the worker walked away and returned to his duties.

"Aw," she said, "I think he was about to show me the right one to buy. Why'd you have to ruin it?" Her eyes twinkled. "Could it be you were getting jealous I was getting so close with him?"

"If that's called getting close, then nobody would make tempura with oranges."

"What are you talking about?"

"I'm just saying something meaningless, so don't think about it too hard."

I'd intended that to annoy her, but instead, a moment passed and she roared in laughter even louder than usual.

For whatever reason, she seemed to be in a particularly good mood as she picked out a single length of rope which she purchased along with a tote bag to hold it. The tote bag had a cutesy drawing of a kitten on it. She hummed and swung the bag as we left the store, and we caught more than a few puzzled looks from the shoppers around us, seemingly—and mistakenly—wondering, *Just how much fun could that home improvement store be, anyway?*

She asked, "What do you want to do next, [Classmate Who Knows My Secret]-kun?"

"Hey," I said, "I'm just following you. I don't have any agenda."

"Really? There isn't anywhere you'd like to go?"

"If I absolutely had to answer, I guess I'd say a bookstore."

"Is there a book you're looking for?"

"No. I don't need a reason. I just like to go to bookstores."

"Huh," she said. "That sounds like it could be some old Swedish saying."

"What are you talking about?"

"I'm just saying something meaningless," she said with a gently mocking laugh, "so don't think about it too hard."

She really was in a good mood. I was just annoyed. Wearing opposite expressions, we went into the mall's large bookstore. I headed straight for the new fiction section, but she didn't come along. It felt great having some alone time again, and I browsed the books with pleasure.

As I looked at the covers and read the beginnings of several books, time passed without me realizing. Anyone who loves books knows the feeling, but I admit not everyone loves books. When I looked at my watch, I felt a little guilty at how much time I'd taken, and I searched the bookstore for my classmate. When I found her, she was happily reading fashion magazines. Even just standing and reading in a store, she had a smile on her face. I thought that was incredible. I loved books, and I didn't do that.

I approached her, and she noticed me before I could say anything. She looked at me, and I apologized.

"I'm sorry. I forgot all about you."

"What a lousy way to apologize! But it's okay, I've been reading. Do you like fashion?"

"Nope," I said. "I don't care what I wear as long as it's normal and doesn't make me stand out."

"That's what I figured. I like fashion. Once I get to college, I'll dress up all the time... But I'll be dead before I make it to college. What's real on the inside is more important than appearances, after all."

"That's not at all what people mean when they say that, you know."

Reflexively, I looked around us to see if anyone was listening. What she'd said was outrageous coming from a high school girl, but no one seemed to have taken the slightest interest.

We didn't buy anything at the bookstore. In fact, we didn't buy anything else that day. After we left, we went into a few other shops that caught her eye—an accessory shop, an eyeglass store—but we simply browsed. In the end, the only things either of us bought were the rope and the kitten tote bag.

We were getting tired from walking, and she suggested we stop in a coffee shop. The café, a national chain, was busy, but we lucked into an open table. She held it down for us while I ordered our drinks; she wanted an iced café au lait, and I got myself an iced coffee. When I brought them back to our table on a tray, my classmate was writing in her *Living with Dying* book.

"Thanks," she said. "How much was it?"

"Don't worry about it. I still owe you for the yakiniku."

"Forget about it. I told you that was my treat. But I suppose I can let you buy my coffee."

She happily put her straw into the glass and began drinking her café au lait. I probably don't need to keep describing everything she did as being done happily—her unfailing positivity infused every movement she made.

She glanced from side to side and said, "To everyone else, I bet we look like we're a couple."

"Whatever we look like, we're not a couple, so they can think what they want."

"That's pretty cold," she stated.

"Every boy and girl together look like a couple if you want to see them that way. No one would look at you and assume you're going to die soon. You said it yourself: What matters isn't how other people judge you, it's what's real on the inside."

She said, "That sounds like something you'd say." She laughed mid-drink, and little puffs of air came out of the bottom of her straw and noisily bubbled up through the glass. "By the way, have you ever had a girlfriend?"

I began standing up. "Well, I'm rested. We should get going."

She grabbed my arm and said, "You haven't taken one sip of your coffee."

The same trick wasn't going to work twice on her. Still, she didn't need to dig her nails into my skin so hard. Maybe she was retaliating for the way I shut down the conversation in the yaki-niku place. I didn't want to pick a fight, so I obediently sat back down.

"Well?" she asked. "Have you had a girlfriend?"

I shrugged. "Who can say?"

"I just realized I don't think I know anything about you."

"Maybe you don't," I said. "I don't like to talk about myself."

"Why not?"

"I don't want to blabber on about things nobody's interested in hearing about. I'm not one of those people who are too concerned with what other people think of them."

"What makes you so sure nobody's interested in hearing about you?" she asked.

"Because *I'm* not interested in other people."

I gazed down at the wood grain of the table and laid out my thoughts as if I was arranging them on its surface.

"The thing about people is they don't really care about anyone but themselves. Sure, there are exceptions. Even I can become interested in someone with remarkable circumstances—like you—but I'm not the sort of remarkable person someone else would be interested in. And I don't feel like talking about something if nobody has anything to gain from it."

This was a long-held belief I usually kept inside myself, locked away in a dust-covered slumber. I'd never had anyone I could talk to about it.

"I'm interested in you," she declared.

But I didn't comprehend what she said. When I brushed away the dust, I had stirred up other memories with it; I was lost in them. Searching for the meaning of her words, I looked up, and what I saw took me by surprise. The girl's expressive face only displayed a single emotion now. It didn't take an expert at reading people to see that she was angry.

I asked, "What's the matter?"

"I'm telling you that *I'm* interested in you. I wouldn't ask someone to hang out with me all day if I wasn't interested in who they were. Don't make a fool out of me."

I couldn't understand what she was saying. I didn't see why she would find me interesting or why she would be mad at me.

I said, "I think you do foolish things every now and then, but I don't think you're a fool."

"Maybe you didn't mean it that way, but you still ruined my good mood."

"Oh, I did?" I said. "I'm sorry."

I apologized even though I didn't know what I'd done to offend her. I wasn't one to shun the most effective way of appeasing an angry person. It worked with her like it did with most other people I'd made mad—she puffed out her cheeks in a pout, but the anger slowly melted from her expression.

"I'll forgive you," she said, "if you'll answer my question."

I looked down again. "I don't think the answer will be particularly entertaining."

"Tell me. I'm interested."

The corners of her lips had turned up into a slight grin. I wasn't ashamed that she had persuaded me to talk, or that I didn't feel like defying her. I was the boat of reeds.

"It might not be the answer you've built up in your mind," I warned her.

"All right, all right, I got it. Now, tell me."

"I can't remember a time since grade school," I said, "where I ever had any friends."

She didn't say anything right away. "You mean like amnesia?"

"I think I was wrong about you. You are a fool."

I wondered which was rarer—amnesia, or someone her age with an incurable, terminal disease. If it was the latter, then maybe what she said wasn't so outlandish. She screwed up her face at me, but I thought she'd look past that remark if I answered her straight.

"I've never had any friends, so of course I've never had a girlfriend."

"You've *never* had any friends? That's not just how it is now?"

"Yeah. Since I'm not interested in other people, I don't know how to make other people interested in me. But it doesn't bother me, anyway. I don't feel like I'm missing out on anything."

"You've never wanted a friend?" she asked.

"I don't know. A friend could be fun, I suppose, but I believe the world inside my books is more fun than the real one, anyway."

"And that's why you're always reading."

"Yeah," I said. "And thus concludes the boring talk. Just to be diplomatic, I'll ask you the same thing: Do you have a boyfriend? If you do, you should go spend time with him instead of me."

"I had one," she said, her voice not betraying sadness. "But I broke up with him a little while ago."

"Because you're dying soon?"

"No. Besides, I wouldn't tell him that. I haven't even told my friends."

Then why had she been so upfront with me at the hospital? The question didn't eat at me, so I didn't ask it. I didn't make a conscious choice not to—I just didn't bother.

She said, "The thing about him—" She interrupted herself. "Oh, you know him, by the way. He's in our class—though I bet if I told you his name, you wouldn't know it." She chuckled. "He's a really good person, but he was terrible to date."

"That can happen sometimes," I said. Not that I'd know.

"It can. So I broke up with him. I wish that God would save

us the trouble and put labels on people from the start—this one is for being friends with, that one is fine to date."

"I'd appreciate that," I said. "But I get the feeling you'd say you enjoy being with people *because* relationships are so complicated."

She laughed and laughed. "That does sound like something I'd say. Yeah, I guess I might think that. All right, I take back what I said about the labels. You understand me, don't you?"

I almost said I didn't, but I stopped myself. I thought maybe I did understand her—and I had an idea why.

"Because we're opposites," I said.

"We're opposites?" she asked.

"Yeah. I figure if it's an idea I would never think, then it might be something you do. I tried one out, and I got it right."

"Tricky. Did you learn to think like that from your books?"

I shrugged. "Maybe."

We were of two opposing viewpoints. Normally, we wouldn't have any need or expectation of having anything to do with each other.

Until just a few months ago, our only connection was that we inhabited the same classroom, and our only point of contact was her raucous laughter springing into my ears. She made such a racket that, despite my disinterest in other people, I immediately recalled her name when I saw her in the hospital that day. Being my opposite, she must have made an impression.

She drank her café au lait while intermittently—and needlessly—offering her reactions ("Yum!"). I drank my black coffee in silence.

"You might be onto something," she said, "about us being opposites. At the yakiniku place, you kept eating flank and sirloin. But the whole point of going to yakiniku is to try different cuts."

"I tried them. I liked them more than I expected to, but I'll stick with normal meat. Deliberately eating a living being's organs—that sounds kind of monstrous, doesn't it? So does dumping all that sugar and milk into coffee, when it's already perfect as it is."

"I don't think our outlook on food matches up."

"Not just about food," I said.

We sat in the coffee shop for about another hour. Nothing else we talked about was of any importance. We didn't talk about life, death, illness, or our time left in this world. So then, what did we talk about? Mostly, she talked about our classmates. I assumed she was trying to get me to take interest in them, but I could safely say her experiment ended in failure.

The attempt was hopeless from the start. I wasn't about to take interest in my classmates or their simplistic love stories. I knew of tales far less boring and mundane. Surely she must have noticed how I felt, as I wasn't the type of person who could hide his boredom. Still, that she tried so hard to sway me was itself of some mild interest. I wouldn't have wasted my efforts like that. Why try hammering a nail into rice?

Then, when we both started feeling like it was time to go, I asked her a question that had been on my mind.

"What are you going to do with that rope? You're not going to kill yourself, right? You said something about a practical joke?"

"That's right, though I won't be around to see how it goes off. You'll have to see for me. I'm going to hint about the rope in my journal. Whoever finds it will get tricked into thinking I must have been so distraught that I considered suicide. That's the prank."

"That's bad taste is what it is."

"It'll be fine, don't worry. I'll be sure to write that it's not true. I won't leave them hanging."

Letting that one pass by, I said, "I'm not sure that makes up for it, but it's better than nothing."

This utterly alien way of thinking had me feeling both exasperated and amused. I wouldn't spare any thought to how people would react after I was dead and gone.

We left the coffee shop and made our way back into the station and its jostling crowds. We got on our train, where we stood and talked a little, then we were back in our town.

We'd both taken our bicycles to the train station, and we retrieved them from the free bicycle parking area and rode back to the school, where we waved and parted ways.

She said, "Talk to you tomorrow." I didn't think we would talk the next day, as we didn't have library duty, but I said, "Sure."

I took the same way home as I always did, and as I would many times again. But something felt odd. An inescapable fear toward death and erasure had stirred up inside me recently, but now the fear had calmed, if only by a little. All day, the impression my classmate gave off had been so far from death. Maybe death seemed less real to me now.

Starting that day, I had just a little bit of trouble believing she was going to die.

At home, I read a book, ate the dinner my mother made, took a bath, drank barley tea in the kitchen, greeted my father back from work, then returned to my room intending to read some more. That was when a text message arrived on my phone. I almost never used my phone to text, and when the message alert chimed, it almost seemed like a marvel. I flipped open the phone and saw the message was from her. I'd forgotten we exchanged numbers for the student librarian program.

I flopped onto my bed and opened the text message. This is what it said:

> I thought I'd try texting you, I wonder if it'll go through. Thanks for hanging out with me today! ✌ I had so much fun. ☺ There's still more I want to do, so I want us to hang out again. ☺ Let's always get along till the day I die. ☺ See you tomorrow!

My first reaction was to realize I'd forgotten to pay her back for the yakiniku. I left a reminder on my phone so I wouldn't forget the next day.

Then I decided to reply to her text, reading what she sent me again.

"Let's always get along," she wrote.

Normally, her little joke about "the day I die" would be what caught my eye, but it was the part before that drew my focus.

Was that true? Were we getting along?

I thought back upon the day, and it seemed like maybe we were.

I was going to reply with the first thought that came into my head, but I decided against it. Something annoyed me about admitting to her that I'd had a little bit of fun, too.

Keeping that thought locked away deep inside, I instead wrote, "See you tomorrow."

Staying in bed, I opened the paperback I'd been reading and wondered what she was doing on the other side of our phones.

Three

A S I SLEPT THROUGH THE NIGHT, someone was murdered
in the next prefecture over. It seemed to be just a random,
senseless killing, and the news was all that played on TV throughout the morning.

Midterm exams or not, you may think the murder would be all
anyone at school was going to talk about, too. Not in my class; they
weren't talking about the exams, either. Instead, their excited mur-
murs were about a different topic—one I rather wished they'd avoid.

It seemed they were trying to solve a mystery: the mystery of
why the bright and cheerful, most popular girl in class would go
out for coffee on a weekend with the class's quietest, gloomiest
boy. I would have liked to know the answer myself, but as usual,
I tried to avoid any unnecessary interactions with my classmates.
I never got the chance to ask if they figured it out.

For a moment, it looked like they reached a consensus:
she and I had gotten together for a student librarian planning

meeting. So far, I hadn't involved myself in the conversations, and I hoped that would be the end of it. Then someone with meddlesome bravery and a lack of restraint asked her directly—and loudly—and the girl answered with something even more meddlesome than that.

"We're getting along."

Being the focus of the class's attention had me listening in a little more closely than I usually did. Now I noticed, but of course pretended I hadn't, that they all kept looking at me

After the first exam, my classmates kept throwing stares my way. I would have liked to know why I had to be under such a cloud of suspicion when I had hardly even spoken to them before, but I continued ignoring them.

I was forced to become involved in the discussion only once; it happened after third period and was quickly resolved.

That meddlesome and inconsiderate girl who'd asked the question before trotted over to me and said, "Hey, [Unremarkable Classmate]-kun, are you being friendly with Sakura?"

When she asked me that question, I thought she must have been a good person. My other classmates surrounded me at a distance, watching me, while sending this one to the frontlines, taking advantage of her open, straightforward nature.

I sympathized with this girl, whose name I couldn't recall, and I answered, "Not really. We just ran into each other yesterday."

The virtuous and honest girl seemed to accept my response at face value and said, "Okay," before returning to the ring of students.

I had no qualms about lying in this situation. To protect

myself—and to preserve my classmate's secret—I saw no other choice. Because our connection was directly linked to her incurable illness, I suspected she would back up my story, no matter how much trouble she typically liked to stir up.

For now, at least, the fuss was over. When the fourth and final hour of testing was over, I felt like I'd done well enough on the exams to land somewhere a little above the class average. I helped clean up the classroom without having to communicate with anyone, then I began packing up my things. With nothing else I needed to do, I planned on going straight home. The nice thing about exams was getting home before the afternoon. I was almost out the classroom door when...

"Wait. Wait up, [Classmate I Can Get Along With]-kun!"

I turned and saw the faces of all my classmates, one smiling from ear to ear, and the rest watching us with suspicion. I wanted to ignore both sets, but I was only going to get away with ignoring the latter. The former was walking toward me, and I waited for her.

She said, "We're supposed to go to the library today. I guess there's some work to do."

I could sense the waves of relief from our other classmates.

"No one said anything to me," I said.

"The librarian told me earlier. Are you busy?"

"I'm not busy, I just—"

"Let's go then. It's not like you're going to study anyway."

I thought that was a rude thing to say, but she wasn't wrong, so I went with her.

I don't care to go into what happened at the library in great detail, but basically, she just wanted to poke fun at me. Earnestly, I asked the librarian what work we had to do, and she and my classmate both just laughed. If it weren't for them, I could have gone straight home, but when the librarian apologized and brought out tea and sweets, I begrudgingly forgave her.

After sipping our tea for a little while, the librarian said she wanted to close up early and chased us out. It was only then I asked my classmate why she had lied to me. I figured it had to have been for a very serious reason.

Instead, she shrugged. "I just like playing tricks on people."

I thought, *Why you little...* But I didn't let the irritation show, because that's exactly what a prankster is expecting to get back. Instead, I decided to get even by tripping her on our way to the shoe racks, but she easily hopped over my foot and raised an eyebrow at me. Her smug look annoyed me even more.

I told her, "Keep on acting like the boy who cried wolf, and you'll get punished for it one day—and I won't mind it at all."

"Is that what happened to my pancreas?" she said. "God must have been watching. You'd better not tell lies yourself, lest you meet my fate."

"There's no rule saying it's okay to lie about every little thing just because your pancreas doesn't work."

"Oh, really? I didn't know. Say, have you eaten lunch yet?"

Trying to put as much of a sting to it as possible, I said, "You know I haven't. You pulled me straight from class."

We reached the shoe racks, and she asked, "What are you doing after this?"

"I'm going to buy some things to eat at the supermarket and go home."

"If you don't have anything already made, come out to eat with me. My parents are gone all day, and they left me lunch money."

As I changed into my outdoor shoes, I considered flatly dismissing her offer, but I didn't have it in me to say no. I'd have to come up with an excuse, and I wasn't sure I could find one. The fact that I had enjoyed spending yesterday with her—just a little bit—didn't help.

She put on her shoes, tapped her foot impatiently, and stretched her arms up high. It was a little cloudy outside, so the sunlight wasn't quite as bright.

"Well?" she asked. "There's somewhere I want to go before I die."

I thought for a moment then said, "If any of our classmates see us again, it'll be a pain."

"Oh! That reminds me," she exclaimed so loud I thought she'd gone crazy. When I looked at her, she scrunched up her face to show her displeasure. "[Classmate I Can Get Along With]-kun, you said we weren't being friendly when you were with me. What else would you call yesterday?"

"Yeah," I admitted, "I said that, but..."

"What did I write you last night? I said, 'let's always get along till the day I die.'"

"What's it matter what I told her? Having everyone staring at me is bad enough. I just wanted to stop them from coming over to talk to me and pry into my business."

"You don't have to lie to them," she said. "Who cares what they think? Didn't you say yesterday that it's what's real on the inside that matters?"

"Yeah, what matters is on the inside. So what's the problem if I make them believe something else?"

"Now we're just going in circles," she said.

"Besides," I explained, "I was taking precautions not to reveal your secret. I wasn't telling pointless lies like you do. If anything, you should be thanking me, not getting mad."

She grumbled and made a sour face, like a child who had thought too hard over something complicated.

"Our outlooks just don't match up," I said.

"Maybe not," she said.

"I'm not just talking about food this time. This seems more deeply rooted."

"Sounds heavy," she said with a big laugh. She seemed to be back in a good mood again. Her simple nature and her quickness to discard bad moods must have been two reasons she had so many friends.

"So," she said, "about lunch."

"I'm fine with going to lunch together, but is it really fine with you? That's just time you could be enjoying with your other friends."

"I wouldn't have asked you if I had other plans. I never double-book. I'm doing something with them tomorrow, anyway. But you're the only one I don't have to hide my secret from. It's easy being with you."

"Like taking a breather," I offered.

"Yeah, like a breather."

"Well, if it's to help you out, then I suppose I can do that much for you."

"Really? Yay."

If going to lunch with her would help her relax, then I didn't have any other choices. Even if our other classmates saw us, I could put up with a little hassle for a worthy cause. She needed a place where she didn't have to keep her secret bottled up, so I could hardly say no, could I?

That was the boat of reeds speaking.

I asked, "Where are we going?"

She squinted up at the sky and breathlessly said, "Paradise."

Would there really be a paradise for her? When we lived in a world that would steal the life from a high school girl, I wasn't sure.

I didn't regret going with her, not right away. The regret came when we stepped foot inside the restaurant. Even in the moment, I recognized any impulse I had to blame her was misdirected. No, I was at fault here. I had avoided contact with others for so long, I lacked the ability to recognize the warning signs. I hadn't realized that when you engaged with other people, sometimes their plans were entirely incompatible with your own, and sometimes you wouldn't find out until it was too late. If I had better crisis management skills, I might have been able to do something about it.

"What's wrong?" she asked. "You don't look happy."

How she looked was plain to see. She could tell I was in distress, and she was enjoying it.

I had just the answer prepared for her question, but saying it wouldn't get me anywhere, so I kept it to myself. All I could do was learn from my failure and do better next time.

This is all a roundabout way of saying another thing I learned that day: I wasn't the type of guy who delighted in being surrounded by girls in a mellow, pastel environment.

Before we went in, she said, "The shortcake here is delicious."

I thought that was a little odd for her to say, but it hadn't set off any alarms. I didn't know what to be wary of, probably because I had never been to a place like this before. I never imagined there were restaurants with such a radical disparity of the sexes. When I looked at the menu our server handed me, there was a little checkmark next to a box that said MEN. Apparently, they had separate menus for guys. I didn't know if it was because a male customer was that much of an anomaly, or if the prices were different for men. I would have believed either.

The restaurant was, specifically, a dessert buffet, which wasn't a thing I knew existed. The place was called Dessert Paradise. In that moment, a fast food joint would have seemed like paradise to me.

I could tell she wasn't going to stop grinning at me until I said something, so I said, "Hey."

"What?" she asked.

"Quit grinning at me like that. Listen, are you trying to fatten yourself up, or are you trying to fatten me up? This is the second all-you-can-eat place in two days."

"Neither. I just want to eat what I want to eat."

"Makes sense. And today it's death by dessert?"

"You got it," she said. "You like desserts, don't you?"

"As long as it doesn't have whipped cream," I said.

"Who doesn't like whipped cream? Well, you can eat the chocolate cake, then. It's really good. They have more than desserts here, too—there's pasta, curry, and *pizza* even." She went out of her way to pronounce pizza with an Italian accent.

"That's good news for me," I said. "But can you just call it pizza like normal? It's grating."

"The parmesan, you mean?"

I wanted to dump parmesan over her goofy head, but I didn't like to inconvenience other people, so out of compassion for the server who would have to clean up after, I didn't do it.

I also didn't want to satisfy her by appearing to be flustered. I acted like I had expected this to happen, and I stood and went to the buffet with her. A typical weekday may have had a smaller crowd, but our school wasn't the only one with exams this week, and the restaurant was bustling with girls from all of the different high schools.

At the buffet, I picked out whatever caught my eye: a few carbs, some salad, ground beef steak, and chicken fingers. When I got back to the table, she was already sitting there looking happy. Her plate had nothing but desserts, and it had a lot. I didn't much care for Western desserts—frosted cakes and fruit fillings and the like. I found them overly sweet, and seeing her plate made me feel a little ill.

About half a minute after she began eating, the girl said, "That murder is really scary."

"Oh good," I said with relief. "I haven't heard a single person talking about that today, and I was beginning to wonder if I'd dreamed the whole story up."

"I think nobody cares about it because it happened in some small town in the middle of nowhere."

"That's a more clinical analysis than I'd expect from you."

Her statement caught me by surprise. I could hardly claim to know her well, but the image of her I'd built in my head wouldn't have said that.

"*I* care about it," she said. "I watched the news. Although I thought, oh, I bet that person didn't think they were going to die before I did."

She looked like she had more to say, but I jumped in. "I'm just going to ask this because anything's possible, but did you know the person who got killed?"

She asked, "Do you think I did?"

"Do you think I think you did?" I replied. "All right, enough of that. Go on."

"I care about what happened, but I think most people just go about their lives not particularly interested in thinking about life and death."

"Sure," I said.

She might have been right. Few people spent their days

consciously aware of life and death. The more I thought about it, the more right she seemed to be. The only people who consistently faced their conceptions of life and death were philosophers, theologians, and artists. Well, them and girls stricken with a fatal illness and the boys who stumbled upon their secrets.

She said, "If there's one good thing about having to confront death, it's that I live each day knowing I'm alive."

"Wiser words have never been spoken," I said, only partly sarcastic.

"I know, right?" She exaggerated a sigh. "Ah, if only everyone could be close to dying."

She stuck out her tongue, punctuating what was meant to come off as a joke, but I took it to be her true feelings. Sometimes, when a person says something, the meaning doesn't lie in the message that was sent, it's in how the listener receives it.

I ate the small portion of spaghetti and marinara sauce I'd put on my heart-shaped plate. The noodles were a little firm, but not all that bad. I realized that, for us, food was like our walks home. We placed an entirely different value on each bite.

Of course, that wasn't the way it should be. I could lose my life the very next day, based on some killer's whim—or if not that, something else. I should have placed the same value on that meal as the girl whose pancreas would soon take her life. Even though I could recognize that truth, I was sure I wouldn't truly understand it until death came for me.

Suddenly she asked, "So, [Classmate I Can Get Along With]-kun, are you interested in girls?"

A dab of whipped cream had planted itself on the tip of her nose. How could someone with that ridiculous face have even considered matters of life and death, let alone offered insight into them? The look was too comical to ruin, and I decided not to tell her.

Instead I said, "What makes you ask that all of a sudden?"

"We're at a restaurant where there're only girls, but it just seems to have thrown you out of sorts. And when a cute one walks by our table, you don't give her a glance. Even *I* take a glance, but not you."

So much for trying not to appear shaken. I resolved to work on my acting ability; I wondered if I could improve before she died.

I replied, "I don't like being somewhere I don't belong, and staring at people is rude. I don't act rude."

"That sounds like you're calling *me* rude," she said, puffing out her cheeks. With the whipped cream still on her nose, this expression was even more amusing than the one before, like the kind of face you'd make on purpose if you were trying to make someone laugh.

"Here's a rude question for you," she said. "You told me yesterday you've never had a girlfriend or a friend. That got me wondering: Have you ever even liked anyone before?"

"It's not that I don't like people. You could say I like everyone."

"Yeah, yeah, I get it. But have you ever *like*-liked anyone?" She sighed and popped a piece of chicken into her mouth. She seemed to be getting acclimated to my twisting of words. "Surely you've had a one-sided crush before. Unrequited love."

"Unrequited love?"

"That's the one that's not requited," she offered.

"Thanks," I said. "I know what it means."

"Okay, talk about it then. Have you ever had a crush?"

I decided making a big deal of it would just be even more of a hassle. I didn't want to anger her like the day before; I was no match for that.

"Maybe once," I said. "I guess."

"That's the spirit. All right, out with it. What was she like?"

"Why do you want to know so bad?"

"I just want to," she said. "You said we're opposites, didn't you? I'm curious what kind of girl you'd like."

I thought about telling her to become her opposite, and then she'd know for herself. But I didn't like pushing my values onto other people, so I didn't say it.

"Let me think," I said. "What kind of girl was she... She added '-san' to everything."

The girl brought her eyebrows together and twitched her nose. The whipped cream moved with it. Confused, she asked, "San?"

"You know, like after people's names, to be polite? But with everyone. She was in my class in junior high, and she'd say book-seller-san, store clerk-san, fish seller-san. She did it with authors' names in our textbooks. Akutagawa-san, Dazai-san, Mishima-san. She even did it with her food. Daikon-san, if you can believe it. Now that I think about it, it might have just been a habit of hers, like a vocal tic that had nothing to do with the kind of person she was. At the time, I thought it meant she held on to respect for the people and things around us. It represented kindness and elegance. Because of that, I felt something a little different for her than I did for anyone else."

Having said all that, I took a drink of water before adding, "I don't know if it counts as unrequited love."

I looked at my classmate; she didn't say a word. She simply smiled and took a bite of her fruit-covered cake. As she chewed, her smile deepened. I was beginning to wonder what she was thinking when she rubbed her finger on her cheek and lowered her head, looking up at me with her eyes.

I asked, "What?"

"Nothing," she said. She wiggled a little bit. "Nothing, it's just, that's sweeter than I was expecting. It's gotten me a little flustered."

"Oh. Well, yeah, I guess she was sweet."

"No, I'm talking about the reason you liked her."

I didn't know how to respond to that, so I copied her and took a bite of my ground beef steak. It tasted good, too. She was watching me with a smile more pleasant than her usual one.

She asked, "What came of it? But I guess you already said—you never had a girlfriend."

"Yeah. Well, in this case, what was on the outside matched the inside. She was cute, and some cheerful, popular guy in my class took her instead."

"Hm. Then she didn't have an eye for people."

"What does that mean?"

"Nothing. Never mind," she said. "So there was a time when you were pure-hearted and stirring with fleeting love."

"Sure," I said. "Just out of courtesy, I'll ask you the same."

"I've had three boyfriends," she replied. "Just to be clear, I took all my relationships seriously. A lot of people say junior high romances are just games, but they're idiots who don't want to take responsibility for their feelings."

She was getting heated, both in her words and her expression. I shrank back a bit. I wasn't good with heat.

For what it was worth, with her looks, I easily believed she'd had three boyfriends. She didn't seem to wear much makeup, and she wasn't some beauty who would make anyone's head turn, but her features were striking.

Seeing me shift, she protested, "Hey, don't pull away."

"I'm not pulling away. But you've got something on your nose. Some whipped cream."

"Huh?" she said, looking foolish as she failed to process it right away. If that was how she looked all the time, she might not have gotten any boyfriends. Finally understanding what I'd said, she scrambled for her napkin and put it to her nose. I stood from my chair before she finished wiping the whipped cream away. I wasn't trying to leave again—my plate was just empty.

Thinking I'd try a little dessert, I got a second plate at the buffet. I was searching around for just the right thing, when, as luck would have it, I found one of my favorite sweets: warabi-mochi, a chilled, jelly-like treat, perfect for the summer. I put a few on my plate and drizzled them with the provided brown sugar syrup, which flowed from the ladle with an artistic beauty. When I broke from my rapture, I decided to get a cup of hot coffee while I was up.

As I weaved my way through the mass of school girls, I tried thinking of how to get her out of her bad mood. What had worked the day before? When I got back to our table, my fears proved false, and she was cheerful again.

But something else kept me from sitting back in my seat.

When my classmate saw me, her smile deepened. The girl who occupied my seat noticed her expression change and turned my way. The second girl's mouth opened in surprise. I recognized her from somewhere.

The other girl said, "S-Sakura, when you said you came here with someone, you meant [Gloomy Classmate]-kun?"

She came off as even more headstrong than my lunch companion. After a moment, I placed her: I'd often seen the two girls doing things together at school. I thought she might have been on one of the sports teams.

"Yes," my companion replied. "Why are you so surprised?" She looked at me and added, "[Classmate I Can Get Along With]-kun, this is my best friend, Kyōko."

She smiled, while her friend looked unsure. I was left holding my dessert and coffee, waiting to see how this interaction would run its course. Part of me would have rather not stuck around to find out, but for the time being, I put my dishes on the table and sat in an open chair. Our table was round, with four chairs, either fortunately or unfortunately, depending on how this went. The two girls faced each other while I sat in the middle, where I could see them both without particularly trying.

"Wait," the other girl said, "so you *are* getting along with [Gloomy Classmate]-kun?"

"Yeah. Surely you heard me say so when Rika asked," she replied, giving me a small grin. Her friend's confusion only deepened.

"But Rika told me you were joking."

"[Classmate I Can Get Along With]-kun just doesn't like that kind of attention, so he misled her. Rika believed him over me— and here I thought she was my friend."

She said it jokingly, but her friend didn't laugh. Instead, the friend turned an appraising gaze upon me. Our eyes met, which caught me off guard. I tried to gloss over it with a quick bow of my head in greeting; she reflexively nodded back at me. For a moment, I thought that would be the end of it, but a real best friend wasn't going to let me off with only a bow.

"Hey," the friend said to me. "Have we ever talked before?"

I thought that was a rude question, but since she didn't seem to mean anything bad by it, I didn't let it bother me.

"We have," I said. "I'm pretty sure it was when I was working the front desk at the library."

My companion, who was listening in, laughed and interjected, "You can't call that talking."

I thought, *That's just your opinion,* but her friend muttered, "I wouldn't." Whatever the case, neither her friend nor I particularly cared what it was called.

"Kyōko, is it all right that you're sitting with us?" the girl asked. "Aren't your friends waiting for you?"

"Oh, right," the friend said. "I was just about to head out. Listen, Sakura, I'm not complaining, but I've got to ask." She glanced at me but otherwise kept her eyes locked on my companion. "You've gone out with him two days in a row, and now you're at this place, alone, where only girls and couples go. So when you say you're getting along, is that what you mean—as a couple?"

"No," she said. I was about to say the same, but she beat me to it, so I held back. Both of us saying it at the same time might have come across as suspect.

The friend's expression softened in relief. But then she frowned again with suspicion as she looked at us in turns.

"Then what are you?" the friend asked. "Friends?"

"It's just what I said. We get along."

"Forget it, Sakura. Sometimes you're impossible, you know." The friend looked at me. She knew—probably from experience— that she wouldn't get any direct answer from my companion. "[Gloomy Classmate]-kun, if I said you two were just friends, would I be right?"

I took a moment to consider how to handle this stray bullet that had been lobbed my way. I chose the best response I had.

"We get along."

I could see both their faces at the same time; one fed up and disgusted, the other beaming with delight.

The friend sighed dramatically, shot my cohort a glare, and said, "I'll get to the bottom of this tomorrow." She waved goodbye to her—and not me—and left.

I wondered if my companion's plans for the next day were with this friend. It made me a little gleeful to think of her being put in the line of fire tomorrow instead of me. I'd given up on caring about the rest of the class staring at me. As long as it never came to real harm, I could ignore it.

Sounding half surprised and half happy, the girl said, "I can't believe we ran into Kyōko here." She plucked a warabi-mochi from my plate without asking. "We've been friends since junior high. She's always been strong-willed, so I was intimidated by her at first, but as soon as we started talking, we hit it off right away. She's a good girl, [Boy I'm Getting along With]-kun—you should try to get along with her, too."

I paused, then took a deep breath and said, "Are you sure it's all right not to tell your best friend that you're sick?"

I knew I was going to spoil the moment by saying that. If her upbeat mood could be likened to bright, happy colors, this was dumping a bucket of ice water, washing the colors away to a dull gray.

But I didn't mean it to deliberately hurt her.

For once, I was being thoughtful and sympathetic. What I was really asking, without any other motive behind it, was if she really should be spending her limited time with me, of all people. Wouldn't her final days be better shared with her best friend, someone who surely meant vastly more to her than me?

"Yeah, it's all right," she said confidently. "That girl gets emotional. If I told her, she'd probably start bawling every time she saw me. Where's the fun in spending time like that? I've already made up my mind: For my own sake, I'm hiding this from every-one until the last possible moment."

Her manner and expression remained upbeat, as if she had repelled my splash of ice water through sheer force of will. I de-cided not to ask anything like that again.

But this show of determination had another consequence. A doubt that had been dormant inside me since the day before now came bubbling up to the surface. I needed to ask.

"Hey, listen," I said.

"What?" she asked.

"Are you really dying?"

Her expression faded in an instant, and I immediately wished I hadn't asked. But before that regret had a chance to linger, her expression came back, quickly cycling through a range of emo-tions as it had before.

First it was a smile, then she looked upset, then a bittersweet grin, then anger, then sadness, then upset again. Finally, she looked me straight in the eye, smiled, and said, "I'm dying."

"Ah," I said.

Her smile deepened, and she blinked faster than usual. "I've known I was dying for years now. I guess thanks to medical ad-vancements, my illness doesn't show, and I've been able to live longer than I otherwise would have. But I'm dying. They tell me I might have another year left, or I might not."

She was saying things I didn't want to know, and that I didn't want to hear, but I was still listening.

"You're the only one I'll tell, [Boy I'm Getting along With]-kun.

You're the only one who can give me reality and normalcy. The doctors can only offer me reality. My family overreacts to everything I say, and they can barely, desperately hold on to a thin veneer of normalcy. If my friends knew, I think they'd be the same way. You're the only one who's able to know the truth and still let me be normal. I can enjoy being with you."

I felt a sting of pain, like a needle driven into the back of my heart. What hurt was knowing I could give her no such thing. If I had anything to offer her at all, it was an escape, and I wasn't sure I even gave her that.

I said, "Like I told you before, I'm not that special."

"Whatever," she said. "Don't you think we must look like a couple?"

"What do you mean by that?"

"I'm just saying." She cheerfully put a forkful of chocolate cake into her mouth. She really didn't look like someone who was going to die soon.

That's when I realized—

Nobody outside a terminal ward looks like they're going to die. Me, her, that person who got killed the day before—we were all alive yesterday. We were living our lives, not behaving as if we were going to die. Maybe that's what it meant to value every day the same.

I was lost in my thoughts when she scolded me, "Don't look so serious. You're going to die, too. We'll meet again in heaven."

"You're right," I said.

Getting emotional over her life was conceited. I'd been arrogant to believe I was guaranteed to outlive her.

She said, "So you'd better be like me and stock up on good deeds."

"Maybe I'll take up Buddhism after you die."

"And just because I'm dead, don't think I'll let you get away being with another girl!"

"Sorry," I said. "You're just a casual fling."

She roared that delighted laugh.

We stuffed ourselves with all the food we wanted, then paid separately, left the restaurant, and decided to go home for the day. Dessert Paradise was a bit of a walk from our school; typically, I'd have covered that distance by bike, but going to our respective homes to retrieve our bikes would have taken too much time and effort, and she had suggested we walk straight to the restaurant, still in our school uniforms.

On our way back, we walked briskly on the sidewalk along the main road together. The sun was out, though no longer directly overhead.

"Hot weather can be nice sometimes," she said. "This could be my last summer, so I'd better enjoy it to the fullest. I wonder what we should do next... When you hear summer, what's the first thing you picture?"

"Watermelon popsicles," I replied.

She laughed. I was getting the idea she laughed a lot.

"Besides watermelon," she said. "What else?"

"Shaved ice."

"That's, like, the same thing!"

"All right," I said, "when you hear summer, what do you think?"

"The usual things, I guess: the seaside, fireworks, festivals. A summer's *aventure!*" The accent was back, although this time it was French.

"Are we going hunting for gold?"

"Gold? What are you talking about?"

I explained, *"Aventure*—that's French for 'adventure,' isn't it?"

She affected a sigh and turned both palms to the sky as she shook her head. Making a display of being disgusted with me was one thing, but what an annoying way of doing it.

"Not that kind of adventure," she said. "Come on. Summer, adventure; you know what I'm talking about."

"Waking up early and going bug catching?"

"That settles it. You're an idiot."

I replied, "I think it's a bigger idiot who gets romance in her head just because the season changed."

"So you *did* know what I was talking about! Agh!"

She glared at me. I was sweating enough already, so I reflexively looked away.

She said, "Can you stop being so difficult and quit dragging this out longer than it has to be? It's too hot out."

"I thought you said the heat was nice."

She pushed past my remark. "A summer's fleeting romance. A summer's mistake. I'm a teenage girl, so I figure I ought to have one or two of those, right?"

Fleeting or not, a mistake didn't sound like a very good idea to me.

"As long as I'm still alive," she said, "I should experience love."

"You've had three boyfriends already. Haven't you experienced it enough?"

"The heart isn't measured by a number," she said.

"That's one of those things that sounds deep at first, but if you think about it a while, it doesn't make any sense. What you really mean is, you want another boyfriend."

I'd said that lightly enough, but if I expected her to respond with another joke, I was wrong.

She stopped walking and stood still, as if struck by a thought. Since she'd done so without warning, my momentum carried me another five steps before I turned to see why she had stopped. I wondered if maybe she saw a hundred-yen coin on the ground or something, but no, her eyes were locked on me. She'd moved her arms behind her back, and her long hair fluttered in the breeze.

"What is it?" I asked.

"If I said I really did want another boyfriend, how far would you go to help me?"

She looked as if she was testing me, like she was trying to make her expression deeply meaningful.

As for what that expression meant, or what her words meant, I was too unaccustomed to being around other people to know.

"How far would I go?"

"Never mind," she said, shaking her head. "It's all right."

She started walking again. When we were side-by-side, I glanced over to see her expression, but it had reset to her usual happy face, which left me even further away from any understanding.

"Was that a joke?" I asked. "Like, were you going to ask if I could set you up with one of my nonexistent friends?"

"No, that wasn't it," she said, flatly refuting the only explanation I could think of.

"Well, what did you mean?" I asked.

"It doesn't matter. Life isn't a novel—if you think everything I say has to mean something, you're seriously mistaken. It didn't mean anything. You should really spend some more time around people, you know."

"Oh, okay."

Apparently, I was supposed to accept that, but it didn't make sense to me. If her question didn't mean anything, then why did she say my guess was wrong? But the boat of reeds didn't raise the point. Something about her manner signaled we were finished talking about the matter, though with my inexperience, I couldn't be sure if I was picking up on the right message.

When we parted ways outside our school, she waved goodbye to me and called, "I'll let you know when I've come up with the next plan."

I didn't bother asking when I'd lost any say in the matter. Instead, I waved back and turned to go. If you've already eaten the poison, you may as well lick the plate.

All the way back home, I thought about our bewildering exchange, but I came no closer to understanding what she'd meant.

I figured I'd be dead before I understood.

Four

I INTERPRETED *LIVING WITH DYING* not as a journal, but as an account of her life; a record of the things she did and felt so they would remain after she was gone. From what I gathered, she'd come up with a set of rules, a framework for what she would and wouldn't document.

The ones I knew were as follows:

First, she didn't write in it every day. She only included days where something special happened, or when she felt something special; something she considered worthy of leaving a remnant behind.

Second, *Living with Dying* only contained written words. She seemed to regard things like pictures or graphs as being out of place in the paperback-like book. On its pages, she wrote prose in black ink and nothing else.

Third, she had decided to keep her book private until after her death. As long as she was alive, her writings were for no one's eyes but hers—except for the single page revealed to me through her carelessness.

She instructed her parents to make the book available, after her death, to everyone who was close to her. Whatever her current use of the book was—whether she considered it a diary or anything else—if it was to be passed on and read after her death, then from my point of view, the book wasn't a journal, but a memoir, or would become one after her passing.

While she was alive, her writings weren't meant to impart an influence or be influenced by anyone. But just once, I asked her to change it for me.

I told her I didn't want her to write my name anywhere in her book. My reason was simple: I didn't want to be unnecessarily hassled or pried by her family and friends once they read it.

One day, as we were working in the library, she told me, "All kinds of people show up in my book." When I requested she leave my name out, she said, "It's my book, and I can write what I want." She had a point, so I didn't fight it. Then she added, "Telling me you don't want me to just makes me want to do it more."

I resigned myself to the hassle that would follow her death.

I thought my name might have possibly made an appearance alongside the yakiniku and the dessert buffet, but the two days that followed were free of that danger.

That was because, for those two days, we didn't speak at school. There wasn't anything weird about it, our typical routines just didn't give us any cause to interact. If anything, the days where we went out to eat together were the anomalies.

I went to school, took my exams, and quietly went home. Every now and then I felt the eyes of her friends and her social group upon me, but I decided I didn't need to let that bother me.

For two days, nothing truly special happened. If I had to, I could think of two minor incidents. The first was when I was sweeping the hallway at school in silence.

A male classmate, who typically never even gave me a glance, came up to me and said, "Yo, [Unremarkable Classmate], are you dating Yamauchi?"

His bluntness was almost refreshing. For a moment, I suspected he might be mad at me because he had a thing for her and misunderstood what was going on. But from his demeanor I surmised he wasn't. His expression was cheerful, unclouded by any hostility. He seemed like a big ball of impulsive curiosity.

"No," I replied. "Definitely not."

"Really? But you guys went on a date, didn't you?"

"We just happened to go out for lunch, that's all."

"What, really?"

"Why do you care so much?" I asked.

"Huh?" he replied. "Oh, you don't think I *like* her or somethin', do ya? No way! I'm into the quieter types."

I hadn't asked, but that hadn't dissuaded him from blabbering away without a care. At least we agreed on one point: She wasn't a quiet type.

He said, "So I heard wrong, then. The whole class is talkin' about it, you know."

"They're wrong. Let them talk."

Then he asked, "Oh! Hey, you want any gum?"

"No," I said. "But could you bring me the dustpan?"

"On it."

I thought he'd say no, seeing as he always slacked off when it was time to clean up, but to my surprise, he did as I'd asked with no fuss. Maybe he just didn't get the general concept of our school cleaning time, and all he needed was to be told what to do.

He didn't ask me any other questions after that. And that was the first unusual event of those two days.

Talking to that classmate hadn't been a good or bad experience, but the second unusual event—minor as it was—put me in a slightly depressed mood.

The bookmark I'd inserted into my current book went missing.

Luckily, I remembered my place without it, but the bookmark wasn't one of the free ones handed out at bookstores, it was a thin and plastic souvenir from a museum. I didn't know when I'd lost it, but my own carelessness must have been at fault. I didn't have anyone to blame, and for the first time in a while, I felt down.

And so, aside from feeling down about something that was ultimately trivial, those two days were normal. Normal for me was peaceful, which meant I didn't have a dying girl hanging around me.

The prologue to the destruction of my respite came on Wednesday night. I was thoroughly enjoying my return to normalcy when the text message arrived.

Even after I read it, I didn't realize the full extent of the disruption about to occur. Whether I liked it or not, I was a character in this new story, and the first chapter was coming. Only the reader could flip ahead and see where the chapter was set. The characters knew nothing.

This was the message:

> We made it through the exams! No test and no school tomorrow! 😊 So... Are you free tomorrow? You're free, aren't you. I'm thinking we should go on a long train trip! ✌
> Is there anywhere you want to go?

I felt a little insulted she would just assume I didn't have any plans, but she was right—I didn't—so I had no excuse to turn her down.

I replied, "If there's anywhere you want to go before you die, we can go there."

Of course, that would come back to bite me. By then I should have known handing over all decision-making to her was a bad idea.

She sent me another message telling me when and where to meet her. The place was a major train station in our prefecture, a hub through which many lines came and went. The time was a little early, but I assumed she'd chosen it on a whim, and I thought nothing of it.

I sent back "OK" and her reply came back immediately. It was her last of the night.

You'd better not go back on your word, you hear?

I wasn't the type of person who would stand anyone up—not even her—so I replied, "Don't worry," and set my phone down on my desk.

This may count as a spoiler, but the way she phrased it— "You'd better not go back on your word"—was a trap. Or at least, that's how I came to view it. I thought she was referring to my agreement of going on a trip with her. What she was really referring to was the thing I never should have said in the first place— that we could go *anywhere* she wanted to go before she died.

The next day, when I arrived at our early morning meeting point, she was already there, wearing a large, sky blue backpack and a straw hat, neither of which I'd seen her wear before. She looked like she was about to go on vacation.

Before we'd even said hello, she noticed me, and her eyes widened with shock.

"Where are all your things?" she asked. "Is *that* all you're bringing? What about your change of clothes?"

"My change of clothes?" I repeated dumbly.

"Well, it'll be okay. We'll just have to buy you clothes when we get there. I'm sure there'll be a Uniqlo or something."

"'There'? Uniqlo? What?"

I started feeling unsettled.

Paying no attention to my apprehensive questions, she casually looked at her watch and asked, "Have you had breakfast?"

"Some toast, but that's all."

"I haven't. You mind coming with me to buy something?"

I didn't and said as much. She flashed me a grin and began walking briskly through the station's shopping area to the place she had in mind. I thought she might be looking for a convenience store for a little snack, but instead we arrived at a place that sold boxed bento meals.

I asked, "You're buying a bento meal?"

"Sure. We're allowed to eat on the bullet train, you know. Do you want one?"

"Wait, wait wait wait wait," I said.

She was happily gazing at the storefront display case where an assortment of takeout meals had been carefully arranged. I took her by both of her arms and pulled her away from the order counter. The old woman behind the counter watched us, seemingly finding us cute.

When we were face-to-face, I was surprised to see her expression—one of surprise.

I said, "That's what I'm supposed to look like right now."

"What's wrong?" she asked.

"First the bento, then the bullet train? I need you to tell me what you're planning today."

"A long train trip. You know, like I texted you about?"

"And by train you meant the *bullet train?* Just how long is this trip anyway?"

She looked like she just remembered something, then reached into her pocket and retrieved two rectangular slips of paper: train tickets.

She handed me one. When I read it, my eyes widened in shock.

"This is a joke, right?" I said.

She laughed. Not a joke, it seemed.

I said, "Come on, that's too far for a day trip. We need to come up with a new plan."

"Oh no, [Boy I'm Getting along With]-kun, you've got it all wrong."

"Ah, good. So this *is* a joke."

"No. It's not a day trip."

I blinked. "What?"

The rest of our conversation went nowhere, and she overpowered me in the end. Here's the short version; that should be enough:

She insisted, I tried to persuade her, she brought out my text from the night before, and she took advantage of my unwillingness to break my word.

The next thing I knew, we were on the bullet train.

Sitting in the window seat, I sighed. As I watched the landscape gliding by outside, I tried to decide if I should just accept my situation now that I was already in it. Next to me, she was enjoying her mixed rice.

She said, "I've never been to Fukuoka before. Have you?"

"I haven't."

"Don't you worry, I bought us a guide book."

"Oh, okay."

I cursed myself; surely even a boat of reeds should have its limits.

Making matters worse, she'd paid for my ticket like she'd paid for my yakiniku. She told me not to worry about it, but I committed myself to repay her no matter the personal cost.

I was thinking about getting a part time job when she thrust a mandarin orange in front of my face.

"Want one?" she asked.

"Sure. Thanks." I took the orange and peeled it without another word.

"You seem down," she said. "Don't tell me you're not on board with this."

"I'm on board with your plan and this train. I'm just taking a long hard look at myself."

"Don't be so depressing. This is a trip. You've got to cheer up!"

"I'd say this is less a trip and more like an abduction."

"Instead of looking at yourself," she said, "you should look at me."

I said, "I don't know what you're talking about."

She seemed to decide on ignoring that. Finished with her bento meal, she put the lid back on and slipped a rubber band around the plastic container to keep it closed. Her brisk movements seemed very alive.

I didn't feel like remarking on the difference between the vibrant image she projected and the reality underneath. Instead, I quietly ate the orange one wedge at a time. The fruit was surprisingly sweet and delicious for something bought at a train station kiosk. I looked out my window and saw an unfamiliar vista of wide open, rural countryside. A scarecrow stood in one of the fields. I don't know why, but at that moment, I decided that, if I'd already chosen to come on the trip, there was no point in continuing to fight it.

She was reading up on local specialties in a travel magazine when she suddenly asked, "By the way, [Boy I'm Getting along With]-kun, what's your first name?"

Gazing at the wooded mountains in the distance had put me in a tranquil mood, so I answered without any fuss. My name isn't particularly unusual, but she nodded her head several times with deep interest. Softly, she said my full name to herself.

Then she said, "Isn't there an author with a name like yours?"

"Yeah," I answered, "although I don't know which one you're thinking of."

Both my family name and my given name were similar to that of one of two novelists.

She asked, "Is that why you like reading so much?"

"Yes and no. It's why I started reading, but I like reading because I enjoy it."

"Is your favorite writer one with your name?"

"No. My favorite is Dazai Osamu."

When I said the name of a great literary master, the girl's eyes widened with some surprise. "Isn't that the guy who wrote *No Longer Human?*"

"That's him."

"That book is kind of dark, isn't it? Is that what you like?"

"It's true that Dazai's brooding nature comes through in the novel's atmosphere, but I don't know if I would simply call it dark."

For once I was speaking with excitement, but she pouted her lips in disinterest and said, "Hmmm, well, it still doesn't sound like something I want to read."

"You don't seem that interested in reading books at all."

"Yeah, not really. I read manga, though."

I'd figured as much. Not in a judgmental way; I just couldn't picture her sitting still long enough to read a novel. Even when she read manga in her room, I imagined she did so moving around and making verbal reactions through the whole thing.

Seeing little point in talking about a topic that didn't interest her, I instead asked a question that was on my mind.

"It must have been some trick getting your parents to let you go on this trip. How'd you pull it off?"

"I told them I was going with Kyōko. If I tell my parents it's something I want to do before I die, they'll get all teary and will pretty much let me do anything. But a trip with a *boy*... They just wouldn't understand."

"That's low, taking advantage of your parents' emotions like that."

"How about you?" she asked. "What excuse did you give your parents?"

"They think I have friends. I've been lying to them about not having any so they won't worry about me. I told them I'm staying at a friend's house tonight."

"That's low, and sad, too."

"It's not hurting anyone. You could at least give me credit for that."

She shook her head with exasperation and took out a

magazine from the backpack at her feet. I didn't think that was a fair way to act when, by instigating this trip, she was the one who put me in the position of having to deceive my parents, whom I loved very much. Anyway, with her opening a magazine, I saw my chance to retrieve a paperback from my school bag. The morning, as turbulent as it was unusual, had exhausted me, and I focused myself on the story to find some relief.

As soon as I opened the book, I immediately suspected her inevitable intrusion upon my peace and quiet. I now inhabited a constant state of suspicion, though whose fault that was I won't say. Contrary to my premonition, this valuable personal time passed by without disruption, and it was only when I reached a stopping place that I realized I'd obtained a precious, tranquil hour of reading. I looked to my side and saw her blissfully sleeping with the magazine against her stomach.

I looked at her face in slumber and saw nothing of the illness that lurked inside. I got the notion to write on her face with a marker but decided to spare her.

She didn't wake up before our bullet train reached our destination, and she didn't wake up once we got there, either.

I don't mean to suggest her short life had expired on the train that day, she simply was in a deep sleep. Please try not to jump to such an inauspicious conclusion.

I gently pinched her cheek and her nose, but she mumbled something unintelligible and didn't wake. As a last resort, I smacked her on the back of her hand with a rubber eraser, and she leaped to her feet in comical overreaction.

She shouted, "How about you try calling my name first!"

She punched my shoulder.

Can you believe that? After I did her the favor of waking her up.

Luckily this was the train's last stop, and we were able to leisurely collect our belongings and disembark.

"We made it!" she said. "Wow! I can smell the ramen already."

"I'm pretty sure you're just imagining that."

"No, I'm sure of it. Has your nose gone bad?"

Not too harshly, I said, "Hey, at least my mind hasn't gone bad like yours."

"Actually, it's my pancreas that's gone bad."

"That's a dirty trick. You can't play that card to win every time. It's not fair."

She laughed and said, "If you don't like it, you should come up with your own."

I wasn't planning on getting an incurable disease in the near future, so I politely declined.

We rode a long escalator down from the railway platform and emerged onto a wide corridor lined with gift shops and waiting areas. The space was pleasant, with that crisp cleanliness of a newly constructed building (whether the space was, in fact, a new addition or not, I didn't know).

A second escalator took us to ground level, where we finally passed through the exit turnstiles. In that moment, I experienced something that left me shaken and questioning my senses. Just as my companion had said, I could smell the ramen. If this smell was real, then what did that mean for other prefectures known for their local cuisine? Did one smell like tonkatsu sauce, and another like udon noodles? Lacking the necessary travel experience, I couldn't deny the notion outright, but I still found it hard to believe a single food dish could so thoroughly seep its way into daily life.

Without looking, I could perfectly imagine my classmate's smug grin. I made a conscious decision not to confirm it.

"So," I said, "where to?"

"Mhm," she said with a knowing cackle. How annoying. "Where to? We're going to visit the shrine of the god of education. But first, we need lunch."

Now that she mentioned it, I was getting hungry.

She said, "I was thinking the obvious—ramen."

"No objection here," I replied.

I followed her as she walked briskly through the bustling train station. She seemed to know right where she was going; she must have decided on a restaurant from the magazine she read on the bullet train. We took a staircase down which led directly to an underground mall. The signature aroma of ramen grew stronger as we walked down the stairs. Sooner than I expected, we were standing in front of the restaurant. It wasn't the most glamorous location, and I started to question if this was the right choice, but I saw a page from a famous gourmet manga in which the restaurant had been featured taped to the wall. I felt reassured we weren't going into some sketchy place.

The ramen was delicious. Our orders came out quickly, and

we greedily devoured the noodles and soup. We both took advantage of the option to order a second helping, and when the waitress asked how we wanted our noodles, my companion said, "Like metal wire," I politely went along with the gag. No one needs to know how embarrassed I became when that turned out to be an actual way people could order noodles. When the stiff noodles came, I imagined the cooking process must have been something like cutting kneaded wheat flour into thin strips and splashing them with hot water.

Fortified by our meal, we went straight back into the station and boarded a local train. The shrine where the god of education resided was only about thirty minutes away. We had no need to rush, but she was running this expedition, and if she said to hurry, I hurried.

On the train, I recalled something I once read. My lips tight, I said, "This is a dangerous prefecture—we'd better be careful. I heard they have shootings here."

"Really?" she said. "That can happen anywhere. Take that murder just a prefecture away from ours."

"I noticed they dropped it from the news."

"I saw an interview with a policeman on TV," she said. "He said random killers are the hardest to catch. Isn't there a saying about how weeds grow faster than grass?"

"I think a murderer is on a different level."

She grinned and said, "I guess that saying also explains why you'll survive and I'll die."

"You know, I just realized something. You can't trust a proverb."

Thirty minutes later, we arrived at our destination. The sky was clear when I could have used a few clouds to turn away the sun's heat. Even just standing there was making me vaguely sweaty. Up until this point, I'd thought I may get away without a change of clothes, but now Uniqlo was looking like a better idea.

"What beautiful weather!" she said. It was hard to say which was beaming more, her face, or the sun. With a buoyant step, she climbed the sloped, pedestrian-only street leading up to the shrine. The pilgrimage road was more crowded than I'd expected for a weekday afternoon. The street—lined on both sides by souvenir shops, various other stores, restaurants, and even one place that sold oddball T-shirts—offered no shortage of interesting sights. The shops selling a local bean cake snack particularly caught my eye, and my nose, as well.

Occasionally, one or another of the stores lured my companion in. We didn't end up buying anything, but the storekeepers didn't expect us to anyway, so we were able to browse without feeling uncomfortable about it.

Sweating, we reached the top of the road leading to the shrine grounds, where the first thing we did was buy drinks from a vending machine. Purchasing from a vending machine that had been so insidiously placed to guarantee a sale, I felt the sting of defeat, but the primal urge to quench my thirst superseded all reason.

She tousled her sweat-streaked hair and grinned. "This is the spring of life!"

"There's nothing like spring about this. It's too hot."

"Have you ever played sports?"

"Nope," I replied. "We of noble birth don't need to exert ourselves."

"Noble, riiight. You should exercise more. You're as sweaty as I am, and I'm sick."

"I don't think a lack of exercise has anything to do with it."

All around us were people sitting in clusters beneath the trees and seeking refuge in their shade. It wasn't just me—the day was especially hot.

Thanks to our refreshments and our youth, we overcame our dehydration and set forth again. We washed our hands at the purification fountain, placed our palms on the hot metal of an ox statue, crossed a bridge over a pond where turtles swam, and finally arrived before the god of the shrine. A stone plaque explained the story behind the ox statue's presence on the shrine grounds, but in the heat, I forgot what it said. My companion never read it in the first place.

I stood in front of the offertory box where the god's money was kept, put in a meager offering, and announced my presence with the customary two bows, two claps, and a third bow.

I read somewhere that shrines weren't places for praying for a wish to be granted; the point was to declare one's determination to the god. But I wasn't determined to do anything at the moment. Since I had to pray about something, I thought I'd help the girl standing next to me. Pretending not to know any better, I prayed to the god for a wish.

May her pancreas be healed.

I noticed she was taking more time with her prayer than I had.

It must be easier to pray for something when you know it won't come true. Maybe she was praying for something else, but I didn't feel like asking her. Prayers should be quietly and privately offered.

When she finished, she said, "I prayed I would be able to stay active until I die. What did you pray for?"

I sighed. "You always have to crush my expectations."

She gasped. "You prayed for me to get weak and infirm? How terrible! I thought you were better than that."

"Why would I wish for something bad to happen?"

My prayer had been for the exact opposite of what she'd guessed, but I didn't tell her. Anyway, wasn't this shrine for the god of education? Then again, a god wouldn't sweat the details.

Then she said, "Hey, let's go get our fortunes!"

I frowned with my eyebrows. A fortune seemed incompatible with her fate; fortunes tell of the future, but she had none.

She trotted over to the counter where the fortunes were sold and dropped a hundred-yen coin into the offering box without skipping a beat. She then drew her number and found the small wooden drawer with the matching fortune. I followed suit out of obligation.

She said, "The winner is the one with the best fortune."

"What do you think fortunes are supposed to be about?" I asked.

"Ah!" she exclaimed. "I got a 'great blessing.'"

Fortunes could fall into categories ranging from great blessing to great curse. She looked happy, while on the inside, I was dumbstruck. What could the god have been thinking? If I ever needed proof that fortunes were nonsense, here it was. Or maybe this unexpected blessing was an act of kindness from a charitable deity.

She burst into loud laugher. "Look at this, look at this! It says my sickness will soon heal. As if!"

I eventually recovered from my stunned silence and said, "I'm glad you're enjoying this."

"What did you get?" she asked.

"Blessing."

"That comes below small blessing, right?"

"Sometimes it's below great blessing. I think it depends on the shrine."

"Either way, I win. Ha ha!"

"I'm glad you're enjoying this," I repeated.

She pointed at my fortune and said, "Look, it says you'll find a suitable marriage partner. Isn't that nice."

"If you really think it's nice, you could sound a little more sincere about it."

She tilted her head, leaned in close, and snickered at me. Caught off guard, I thought, *If she kept her mouth closed, she'd be kind of cute,* and in that moment, I knew I'd utterly lost this round.

I averted my eyes and heard her chuckle, but she didn't say anything more.

We left the courtyard of the shrine's sanctuary and went back the way we came. When we reached the bridge, we turned left instead of crossing and came upon the treasure hall and a second pond, this one called the Iris Pond. A great number of turtles were swimming, so I bought turtle food from a nearby stand and proceeded to toss it into the water. Watching the turtles' leisurely movements, the day seemed to feel a little less hot. While I was absorbed in feeding the turtles, a small girl asked something to my companion, who responded with a pleasant smile. Again, I found myself thinking she was my polar opposite.

"Are you two in love?" the girl had asked.

"No, we're getting along," my classmate answered, to the little girl's confusion.

Once I'd finished feeding the turtles, we walked down a narrow path running along the pond's edge before reaching a little restaurant, an old one-story building with an out-of-place concrete façade. She suggested we go inside, so we did. When the air conditioning hit us, we let out a relaxed sigh in unison. Three other parties occupied tables in the spacious interior: a family, a dignified-looking elderly couple, and a somewhat unruly quartet of middle-aged ladies. We sat at a low table by the window.

Soon after we sat, a genial elderly woman came and filled our glasses with water before taking our order.

My companion said, "We'll each have an umegae mochi, and tea for me." She glanced to me and asked, "You want tea, too?"

I nodded, and the old woman went back to the kitchen with a friendly smile.

As I drank my cold water, I felt my body cool all the way to my fingertips. It felt nice.

I asked, "So those sweets I saw on the road are called umegae mochi, then?"

"They're a local specialty. I read about them in my guide book."

The elderly server returned with two red rectangular trays, each bearing a sweet bean cake and a cup of green tea. "Sorry for the wait," the old woman said, despite there having been no wait at all. Apparently, the policy was to pay up front, so we each handed over our share in coins.

The round, white dumplings were crisp on the outside. Judging from the speed with which they came, the restaurant must have cooked them constantly throughout the day, rather than made-to-order. I took a bite and found it generously stuffed with sweet, slightly salty red bean paste. It was very good, and the green tea matched it well.

"Yum!" my classmate said. "I bet you're glad you came with me now."

"Only a little bit."

"Don't be so stubborn. If you keep being like that, you'll be back to having no friends after I die."

I didn't say anything. I didn't mind the thought of being alone. My current situation was an anomaly since, once she was gone, I would simply return to my previous way of life. I wouldn't interact with anyone, instead immersing myself back in the worlds created in my books. That was what every day had been like for me before, and that's how it would be again. I didn't consider it a bad thing—but I didn't think she was capable of understanding that.

We had finished our umegae mochi and were still working on our tea when she spread open her tourist magazine on our table.

I asked, "What's up next?"

"That's the spirit."

"I already decided I may as well lick the plate, after I saw a scarecrow from the bullet train."

"Oh really? I have no idea what you just said," she said, not stopping to ask. "Here's the thing—I made this list of things I want to do before I die."

I thought that sounded like a good idea. It might help her to realize she had better ways to spend her remaining time than with me.

She explained, "Like going on a trip with a boy, eating tonkotsu ramen here at its home—that's what made me think of doing this trip. I guess the last thing I want out of today is to have motsunabe for dinner." Motsunabe was a local offal-based hot pot stew. "If I can have that, this day will officially go down as a success. What about you? Is there anywhere you want to go?"

"Nope," I said. "I'm not that interested in touristy places, so I wouldn't even know what's here. Like I wrote to you last night: We can just go wherever you'd like."

"Hmmm, well then, what should we—eep!"

She let out a comical yelp. The cause was the sound of shattering ceramics and a woman's undignified shriek. We looked to the source of the sound: One of the four noisy women, the fattest of the bunch, was shouting hysterically. Next to her, the elderly server was bowing apologetically. Apparently, the old woman had tripped or something and dropped a teacup.

I decided to keep watching to see what happened next. The server apologized profusely, but the customer, whose clothes had been splashed by the tea, continued to rage hysterically, her fury building until she seemed to have lost her mind. I looked across the table and saw my companion keeping a close watch on the unfolding scene as she drank her tea.

I hoped the situation would somehow resolve itself peacefully, but such hopes of mine were often dashed. The woman's fury crescendoed as she roughly shoved the elderly server. The server staggered backward into a table before toppling to the ground, overturning the table along with her. Soy sauce bottles and pairs of disposable chopsticks scattered across the floor.

I accepted the course of events and decided to remain a spectator, but my companion didn't.

"Hey!"

She shouted louder than I'd ever heard her before, then she got to her feet and ran up to the raging woman and the woman's posse.

This didn't surprise at all. If I hoped to remain an onlooker, then of course she wanted to become involved. I knew she was going to do this, because that was what my opposite would do.

She helped the fallen server back to her feet while yelling at the woman who was now her sworn enemy. Her foe shouted back, but here's where my companion's true strength came into play. Some of the other diners—the father of the family and the elderly couple—slowly got to their feet and began allying themselves with my classmate.

Beset on all sides, the entire group of middle-aged women—not just the initial offender—hurled complaints as they fled the restaurant with flushed cheeks. The elderly server showered my companion with gratitude and praise, while I was still seated drinking my tea.

My classmate helped restore the toppled table to order before returning to ours. She still looked angry, and I expected she would scold me for remaining on the sidelines, but she didn't.

Instead, she said, "The old lady only tripped because that woman stuck out her foot. How nasty can you get!"

"Yeah," I said. Some people believed bystanders who choose not to intervene are just as guilty as the actual perpetrator. If that was true, it meant I shared equally in the woman's misdeeds, so I didn't criticize her too strongly.

I looked at the girl who was still stoking the flames of her righteous anger, and who had so little time left to live, and I thought, *Weeds grow faster than grass.*

I said, "There are a lot of people out there who should die sooner than you."

"I'll say," she agreed, and I smiled wryly. I reaffirmed my decision to go back to being alone after she was gone.

When we left the restaurant, the old waitress made my companion take six umegae mochi along with her thanks. The girl tried to refuse the gift at first, but she eventually gave in and politely accepted. I tried one, and it was softer than the one before, now that a little time had passed. I enjoyed it this way, too.

My companion said, "Let's go back to the city for now. We need to find a Uniqlo for you, anyway."

"Sure," I said. "I got sweatier than I thought I would. I hate to ask, but could I borrow some money for the clothes? I promise I'll pay you back before you die."

"What? No way," she said.

"You fiend. To hell with you. See if you can find someone to get along with there."

She laughed. "I'm kidding, I'm kidding. That was a joke. And you don't have to pay me back, either."

"No, I'm going to pay you back for everything."

"Stubborn."

We took a train back to the central station. The train was quiet with old people dozing off and a group of little kids plotting their next exploits through hushed whispers. My companion read her magazine next to me while I gazed out the window. It was evening, but the summer sky was still bright. I wouldn't have minded if it always stayed that way. My mind began wandering with such thoughts.

Maybe that would have made for a better prayer, I thought to myself. She closed her magazine then her eyes. She slept the rest of the way.

When we arrived at the station, it was more crowded than in the early afternoon. We walked slowly through the hurrying students and office workers making a quick stop before continuing their commute. The people who lived in this prefecture seemed to walk faster than people in other places. This was a violent prefecture, after all, so maybe they moved quickly to evade trouble.

We talked over what to do and decided to head for the prefecture's largest shopping district. According to my phone, we'd find a Uniqlo there. I later discovered we could have taken a train directly there from the shrine without ever having to exit a station, but given how I'd been abducted, I hadn't the opportunity to do any research ahead of time. She wasn't the sort of person to pay that much attention to the details, anyway.

Instead, we took the subway.

It was already after eight. We sat on small cushions on the restaurant's tatami floor, which was recessed underneath our table so we could stretch our legs out, and we greedily snagged food at our leisure from the shared hot pot between us. Steam rose from the motsunabe stew, a mixture of beef offal, cabbage, and garlic chives that was known around Japan but originated in this region. I would attest that normal cuts are better than offal, hands down, but the motsunabe tasted good enough to keep me from corroborating it at the moment. My companion was more noisy.

"It's good to be alive!" she said.

"That's the truth," I replied.

I drank the broth straight from my bowl; it was rich and delicious.

Before we went to the restaurant, we started at the shopping district where I got clothes at the Uniqlo, then we simply wandered about. She said she wanted to buy some sunglasses, so we went to an eyeglass store. I found a book store, so we went in there, too. Even just taking in the sights of an unfamiliar city's streets was pretty fun. We came upon a park and chased after the pigeons. We tried a famous local confection right where it was made. The time passed faster than we knew.

As night fell, rows of open air food stands set up shop in numbers unseen elsewhere in the country. The cozy, inviting spaces drew our eyes as we walked, but we stuck with her plan and soon arrived at the motsunabe restaurant she'd chosen. Either due to luck or to this being a weekday, we were quickly seated in the busy restaurant.

She boasted, "Good thing I got us in," but she hadn't made a reservation or done anything at all. Whatever the reason we were able to get in, it had nothing to do with her.

During dinner, we didn't talk about anything substantial. She praised the food from start to finish while I quietly munched away. Thanks to the lack of disruptive chatter, I was enjoying my meal to its full extent. Food that good deserved uninterrupted focus.

But soon she opened that disruptive mouth of hers. It was when a server came to deliver the second course, by way of dropping Chinese noodles into our rich and savory broth.

She said, "Now we're two people poking at the same hot pot."

"You mean like two people eating rice from the same pot?"

"It's a step beyond that. I never shared a hot pot with my boyfriend."

Her laugh was higher and louder than normal; that was because now she had alcohol running through her blood. The high-school-aged girl had brazenly ordered a glass of white wine with our meal. She asked for the drink with such confidence that no one working the restaurant questioned her. They could have called the police to save me instead.

She was in an even better mood than usual, and she wanted to talk about herself more than she normally did. That was fine with me; I liked listening to other people talk more than I liked speaking myself.

I don't exactly recall how we got to the subject, but she began talking about her ex-boyfriend who was in our class.

"He's a really good guy. He asked me out, and he was nice and my friend, so I thought, why not? Well, I'll tell you why not. It made everything messy. You know how I tend to speak exactly what's on my mind? Sometimes I'd be a little blunt, and he'd get pissed off right away, and we'd fight, and he just wouldn't let it go. Sometimes you can be fine with someone as a friend, but as soon as you start spending a little more time together, you can't stand them."

She took a drink of wine. I listened quietly, not having any similar experience with which to empathize.

"Kyōko approved of him, too. He's a pleasant guy, on the surface at least."

I said, "He doesn't sound like anybody I'd have reason to get along with."

"Probably not. I mean, Kyōko liked him, but she doesn't want anything to do with you, so what does that say?"

"Aren't you worried saying something like that could hurt my feelings?"

"Did it?" she asked.

"It didn't. I try to stay away from her, too, so the feeling is mutual."

Her tone changed, and she looked at me straight on. "I hope you and Kyōko will be able to get along together after I die."

Since she seemed serious, I acquiesced and said, "I'll think about it."

"Please," she added. That one word carried some weight. I had nearly convinced myself her friend and I would never get along in a million years, but now my confidence in that was shaken. Just a little.

After we'd had our fill of the motsunabe stew, I stepped outside while she paid. I didn't protest, as we'd finally come to an agreement: I would leave all the paying to her, but I would repay later for all my share.

The nighttime breeze felt good on my face. The restaurant was air-conditioned, but the AC couldn't hold its own against the numerous, simmering hot pots.

My companion came out from the restaurant and said, "It feels great out here!"

"At least the night is still cool down south."

"It sure is. Well, I guess we should head to the hotel."

Earlier in the afternoon, I'd asked her where we were staying. It was a fairly high-end place adjacent to the bullet train station, and apparently the hotel was well-known within the prefecture. Originally, she'd planned to get us a couple of rooms at a cheap business hotel, but when she told her parents about it, they pitched in some money, reasoning that if she was insisting on going on a trip, she may as well stay somewhere nice. She didn't fight it. Of course, that meant half the money had been intended for her friend and not for me, but that wasn't my fault.

We arrived at the train station and found the hotel really was right next to it. I hadn't doubted the map, but the place just felt closer in reality than in the abstract.

The only reason I wasn't overwhelmed by the lobby's elegant opulence was because I'd seen pictures in my classmate's travel magazine. If I hadn't come mentally prepared, I might have been dumbstruck and fallen prostrate before her. That would have inflicted a grievous injury to the small shred of self-respect I possessed. Good thing I'd gotten my surprise out of the way with the magazine instead.

Even if I was able to escape getting on my hands and knees, I still felt uneasy amid the setting, which was simply beyond my stature. I left the check-in to her and sat on a sofa in the classy lobby and waited. The sofa was roomy and comfortable.

She strode confidently to the check-in counter like she'd done this many times before, and the hotel staff all bowed to her from their stations. I thought, *No way she's growing up to be a decent, upstanding adult,* but then I remembered she wasn't ever going to be any kind of adult at all.

I drank cold, bottled tea that was as blatantly out of place in these environs as I was. I had a vantage point from off to the side of the check-in counter, and I could watch both sides of the exchange.

At the counter, my companion was helped by a slender young

man with swept-back hair who looked every bit the part of a hotel clerk.

As she began filling out some paperwork, I felt a little sorry for the trouble the receptionist was about to go through in dealing with her. I couldn't hear their conversation, but when she returned the paper to the receptionist, he gave her a pleasant smile, turned to his computer, and began typing. He had good posture. It looked like he found the reservation in the computer, because he turned to her again and spoke to her politely.

But she looked surprised and shook her head from side to side. The receptionist's expression stiffened, and he worked at the computer some more, then spoke again. She shook her head once more, then took her backpack from her shoulders, pulled out a piece of paper from within, and handed it to the man.

He looked back and forth between the paper and the computer monitor before frowning and withdrawing to a back room. She was left there to wait, like I was doing, until the clerk eventually returned with an older gentleman in tow. No sooner had they arrived than they began to bow to her repeatedly.

From that point on, the older man was the one to speak with her, and he did so with apologies written into his every mannerism. She regarded him with an uneasy smile.

As I observed the scene from beginning to end, I speculated as to what was going on. The most reasonable explanation was that the hotel had made an error and failed to properly hold the reservation; but I had trouble reconciling that with her smile. Whatever the case, I decided to remain calm, because in situations like this, the hotel staff were bound to make things right. If we needed to, we could find an internet café or somewhere else to pass the night.

She kept sending me quick glances while holding that uneasy smile. For no particular reason, I nodded to her. I hadn't meant anything by it, but when she saw my nod, she said something to the apologetic hotel staff.

Their faces immediately brightened. They kept on bowing, but this time, they appeared to be thanking her. At the time, I just felt glad everything had been resolved. A few minutes later, I'd want to go back to this moment in time and punch myself. Like I've said many times before, I sorely lacked crisis management skills.

The hotel staff handed her some things—probably the room keys and whatever came with them—and they continued to bow as she approached me. I looked up at her and said, "Looks like they gave you some trouble," as my way of thanks.

She responded with a series of facial expressions. First, she puckered her lips, then looked embarrassed and uncertain, then she looked at me, eyes blinking, as if she were trying to read me. Finally, she replaced all that with a smile.

"Ummm," she said. "So, here's the thing. There was a bit of a mix up."

"Okay," I replied.

"They ran out of the kind of rooms that we booked."

"So that's what that was about."

"Yeah, and...because it was their fault, they gave us an upgrade."

"That sounds nice."

"Yeah, well..." She held out a single room key that dangled from her fingers. "We have to share a room. But that's not a problem, right?"

That took a minute to register, and when it did, all I could say was a tactless, "Huh?"

I won't report the debate that followed, as I was already tired of those myself. Anyone could see where it was headed: She bulldozed me, and we ended up staying in the same room.

But I don't want you to assume it was only because I was weak, or that I was a person of loose morals who didn't think sharing a room with the opposite sex was a big deal. But there was the matter of money, in that she had it and I didn't. I even offered to stay at a different hotel by myself.

But who am I making excuses to?

That's all they were—excuses. I could have taken a stand and gone off on my own, and she wouldn't have been able to forcibly stop me. But that's not what I chose to do. I don't know why I didn't.

In any event, the end result was that we would share a room. But I didn't feel any guilt or shame, and I knew nothing was going to happen that would change that. Our hearts were pure.

Inside the spacious room, she twirled beneath the chandelier's soft glow and said, "I have to admit, I'm nervous about sharing a bed with you. But, like, the fun kind of nervous, you know?"

Well, I was pure, anyway. "Don't be dumb," I said with a scowl.

I walked past the king-sized bed to sit on a couch at the edge of the Western-styled room. Then I told her the obvious.

"I'll sleep here."

"What? Come on, when else are you going to stay in a room as nice as this? You have to experience the bed, too."

"I'll try it out once—when you're not using it."

"Aren't you happy to be able to share a bed with a girl?"

"I'd appreciate if you stopped maligning my character," I said. "I'm a gentleman through and through. If you want to sleep with someone, find a boyfriend."

"Right, you're not my boyfriend—that's what makes it fun. It's like doing something we're not supposed to do."

She seemed to be struck by a thought, and she took *Living with Dying* from her backpack and wrote something in it. I'd often witnessed her doing that.

Then she went to the bathroom and shouted, "Wow! The tub has jets!"

I opened the sliding glass door to the balcony and stepped outside. Our room was on the fifteenth floor, and while it couldn't quite be called a suite, the accommodations were more luxurious than two high schoolers should have been able to experience. The toilet and bathtub had separate rooms, and the balcony provided a magnificent panorama of the nighttime cityscape.

"What a view," she said, having joined me outside without me noticing. Her long hair swayed in the whispering wind. "Looking out at the city at night, just the two of us—doesn't it feel romantic?"

I said nothing and went back inside, where I sat on the sofa, picked up a TV remote from the round table in front of me, and turned on the TV, which was as oversized as the rest of the room.

Most of the channels were playing local shows, different from those I was used to seeing. I found the local dialect and speech patterns of the TV personalities far more interesting than my companion's nonsense.

She came back into the room, closed the sliding door, and crossed in front of me to sit on the bed. "Whoa!" she said. The bed looked plush and very comfortable. I decided trying it out for myself just once wouldn't be such a bad idea.

She settled in on the bedsheets and watched TV with me.

She said, "It's interesting how people talk differently here. They sound like old samurai. It's funny 'cause this city is super modern. I wonder how some ways of talking persist like that." That was certainly more thought-provoking than her usual comments. She added, "I think studying local dialects would be a fun job."

"For once I agree with you," I said. "I've considered doing that sort of research once I'm in college."

With feeling and not in a jokey way, she said, "That sounds really nice. I wanted to go to college, too."

"I don't know what to say to that."

I wished she'd stop saying such things. I didn't know how I was supposed to feel when she did.

She asked, "How about you tell me something cool about dialects? Got any trivia?"

"Let's see... What we hear as the Kansai dialect," I said, referring to the region surrounding Osaka and Kyoto, "might all sound the same to us, but there's actually quite a number of variants. How many do you think there are?"

"Ten thousand!"

"That's ridiculous. It's annoying if you don't even try to guess right. Anyway, there's various opinions, but most people agree there are just under thirty."

"Huh. Is that so."

"You know, I wonder how many people you've hurt in your life."

With how many acquaintances she kept, the true number was likely unfathomable. It was criminal, really. But since I didn't keep any acquaintances myself, I never did anything that would hurt anyone. As for which was the better way to be, I supposed opinions would be divided.

She quietly watched the TV for a while, but then, apparently unable to tolerate being still any longer, she began rolling about on the bed, throwing the sheets into complete disarray. She loudly declared, "I'm taking a bath," went into the bathroom, and began filling the tub with hot water.

With the sound of the rushing water providing background noise from the other side of the wall, she retrieved various small things from her backpack and carried them to the sink, which was located between the bath and toilet rooms. She started running the water there, too, maybe to wash off her makeup; not that I was curious.

When the bathtub had filled, she disappeared happily into the bathroom. She foolishly admonished me, "You'd better not peek," but I didn't even watch her walk out of the room. See, I was a gentleman.

I could hear her humming a vaguely familiar song, maybe

from some commercial or something. How on earth did I get in this situation, being this close to a bathing female classmate? I reflected on the choices and actions that led me here, and whether or not they had been right. I looked up at the ceiling, and I could see the chandelier just in the edge of my view.

I'd made it up to where she punched me on the bullet train when she called my name.

"[Boy I'm Getting along With]-kun," she said, her voice reverberating off the hard walls in the bathroom. "Could you grab me my face wash from my backpack?"

Obeying without thinking into it, I picked up the sky blue backpack from the bed and looked inside.

I wasn't thinking anything at all.

That's why, when I saw what I did, I was rocked as if by an earthquake.

The backpack itself was cheerful, like her.

What was inside shouldn't have disturbed me at all, but my heart began pounding.

I thought I already knew; I thought I already understood. It was the very basis of her presence in my life. But what I saw stole my breath away.

Calm down, I told myself.

Inside the bag were a number of syringes, more pills than I'd ever seen in my life, and some kind of testing machine that I had no idea how to use.

My mind wanted to shut down, but I somehow forced myself to keep thinking.

I already knew her disease was real. I already knew she was only alive through the efforts of medical science. But when I saw the reality with my own eyes, an indescribable terror flooded over me. All my cowardice I'd been keeping bottled up came rushing out.

"What's the matter?" she asked.

I looked over my shoulder and saw her wet arm sticking out from the cracked-open door and gesturing impatiently. She had no idea what I was feeling, and I didn't want her to find out. Quickly, I located the tube of face wash and handed it over.

"Thanks," she said. "Oh, and I'm totally naked right now."

After a moment passed without my reply, she said, "Say something! You're making me embarrassed!"

The door closed.

I walked over to "her" bed and tossed myself onto it; the mattress was as cushy as I had imagined it. The bed engulfed my body, and the white ceiling seemed like it could engulf my consciousness.

I was confused.

But why?

I thought I already knew. I thought I already understood. I thought I had already comprehended it.

But I'd been closing my eyes to her reality.

Just because I saw a few objects, misdirected emotions were trying to rule over me. They were a monster trying to eat at my chest.

Why?

My thoughts spun, trying to find an answer that never came. It was almost dizzying. I closed my eyes and fell asleep on the bed.

I woke to find her gently shaking my shoulders. Her hair was wet. The monster had gone.

She said, "So you *did* want to sleep on the bed."

"I said I'd try it out once, and now I have."

I got up and returned to the couch. Trying as best I could to keep my expression emotionless and the monster's claw marks hidden from her sight, I turned my gaze to the TV. I felt relieved that I had regained enough presence of mind to even make the attempt.

She began drying her long hair with a wall-mounted hair dryer. "You should take a bath, too. The whirlpool jets are amazing."

"I think I will," I said. "No peeking. I remove my human skin whenever I take a bath."

"Did you get sunburned?"

"Sure, call it that if you want."

The clothes I bought with her money were still in the shopping bag, which I brought with me into the bathroom. A sweet scent lingered in the wet air. Ever prudent, I decided to believe it was just my imagination.

I locked the door—just in case—then removed my clothes and took a shower. I washed my hair and body, then got into the tub, turning on the whirlpool jets. My companion hadn't oversold the bath; it felt exquisite. I could feel the monster's footprints being washed away. It was amazing what a good bath could do. I relaxed in the tub for a long time—it would probably be ten or more years before I was ever in a hotel room as nice as this again.

When I emerged from the bath, the chandelier had been turned off and the room was dim. The girl sat on the couch where I was supposed to sleep. A few plastic bags from a convenience store were sitting on the round table in front of the couch.

She said, "I bought some snacks and things from the convenience store downstairs. Could you get us a couple cups from the shelf over there?"

I did as she asked and placed the two glass cups on the table. Since the sofa had been claimed, I sat in a tasteful chair on the opposite side of the table. Like the couch, it was comfy and relaxing.

As I sat there recuperating, she moved the plastic bags to the floor and produced a bottle of amber-colored liquid. She filled each glass about halfway, then topped them up—right to the brim—with a clear carbonated drink from another bottle. She stirred the drinks, completing this mysterious concoction.

I asked, "And this is...?"

"Plum liquor mixed with club soda. I hope I got the amounts right."

"I almost said something at the motsunabe place, but you do know you're still in high school, right?"

"I'm not trying to show off," she said. "I like alcohol. Are you going to have some?"

"Well... I wouldn't want to make you drink alone."

I brought the glass to my lips, careful not to spill. It had been a while since I tasted alcohol. It smelled refreshing but tasted sickly sweet. My drinking partner downed hers, seeming to enjoy every bit of it as much as she said.

She spread out some snacks on the table and asked, "What kind of potato chips do you like? I like them savory."

"Anything but lightly salted is criminal," I said.

"We *really* don't have the same outlooks, do we? And here I only bought consommé flavor. Sucks for you."

I looked at her enjoying herself and took another drink. It was still too sweet. I'd had a fairly large dinner, but snacks have a way of summoning an appetite. I crunched on the heretical chips and tipped back my glass again.

After we both finished our drinks, she made us seconds and proposed the following.

"Let's play a game."

"A game? Like shogi?"

"I barely know how all the pieces move. I bet you're good at it, though."

"I like shogi puzzles where the pieces are laid out and you have to figure out the winning moves," I said. "I can play those on my own."

"Sounds lonely. I brought cards."

She walked to the bed and retrieved a deck of cards from her backpack.

I said, "A card game with two people—*that's* what I would call lonely. Tell me what game you're thinking."

"President?"

"With all the revolutions, there'll be no citizens left to survive."

She laughed, then hummed in thought and pulled the cards free from their plastic carton. She shuffled them, swaying her body side to side as if she was thinking about something. I didn't interrupt her, instead choosing to eat a stick of Pocky from the table.

After she shuffled the deck about five times, she stopped. She seemed to have come up with an idea she liked, as she nodded to herself in approval and turned her glittering eyes to me.

"We're drinking," she said, "so let's run with it. How about truth or dare?"

I squinted. I didn't recognize the name. "What's that?" I asked. "Sounds philosophical."

"You've never heard of it? I'll teach you the rules as we go. The first rule is the most important: You can't quit the game early. All right?"

"If I agree to that, it's like agreeing not to flip over the board while playing shogi, right? All right, I won't quit the game. I wouldn't be so uncivilized anyway."

"Okay, you said it," she said with a mischievous grin.

She moved the snacks from the table to the carpet and deftly spread out the cards face down in the shape of a ring on the table. She was obviously making a show of force, an attempt to intimidate me using our gap in experience—I could see it plain on her face. That gave me all the fire I needed to knock her down a peg or two. This was going to be fine. Card games almost always came down to thinking and luck. As long as I could follow the rules, experience wouldn't matter.

She said, "We'll use these cards since they're handy, but rock-paper-scissors would work just the same."

"I'll take my fire back."

"I already ate it. Okay, let's start. Pick one card and flip it over in the middle of the circle. The bigger number wins. The winner gets privileges."

"What kind of privileges?"

"They get to ask truth or dare. Oh, and we should set the number of rounds. Let's go with ten. Now, pick a card."

I picked a card and turned it over: It was the eight of spades.

I asked, "What if we draw the same number of a different suit?"

"Don't overthink it. We'll just draw again. Just to be clear, I'm making this part up. It doesn't have much to do with the actual game."

She took another drink and flipped a card: jack of hearts. I didn't know what was going on, but losing the draw surely put me at a disadvantage. I remained on my guard.

"Yay," she said. "I get to ask. I'm going to say, 'Truth or dare?' and you say, 'Truth.' Okay. Truth or dare?"

Hesitantly, I said, "Truth... Now what?"

"We'll start with... Who do you think is the cutest girl in our class?"

The question was so out of the blue it took me a moment to react. "What are you talking about?"

"Aren't you following? It's called truth or dare. If you don't want to answer, you can choose dare instead. Then I'll dare you to do something. You have to do one or the other—the truth or the dare—no matter what."

"That's awful. Who came up with this?"

"Don't forget, you can't quit before we're finished, either. You agreed. You wouldn't want to be uncivilized, would you?"

She gave me an awful smirk and took another drink. I kept my expression neutral. I wouldn't give her the pleasure of seeing that she was annoying me.

No, I told myself, *don't give in so fast.* There must be something I can say to get out of this.

I tried, "Is this an actual game? Or did you just invent it right now? I said I wouldn't quit the *game*—if it's not a real one, then it doesn't count."

"Do you really think I'd leave you with such an easy way out?"

"I do."

"I'm sorry to tell you that it's a real, legit game. I saw it in a movie once, and I looked it up. It's been in a lot of movies, actually. But I appreciate you giving me your word a second time now—that you won't quit."

Her laugh belonged to a devil, and her eyes glimmered with wicked intentions.

She had ensnared me again. How many times did this make now?

"Let's keep this clean, all right?" she teased. "When it's your turn to ask me truth or dare, you'd better keep that mind out of the gutter."

"Shuddup," I said.

"Jerk!" she said.

She downed the rest of her glass and began making herself a third. Judging by the half-grin she now wore, the booze must have been taking effect. For my part, my cheeks already felt hot.

"Back to the game," she said. "My question was: Who do you think is the cutest girl in our class?"

"I don't judge people by their looks."

"I'm not asking you to judge them as people. I was just wondering whose face you find the prettiest."

I didn't say anything.

"Let me add," she said, "if you choose a dare instead, I won't go easy on you."

I didn't see anything good coming from that.

I tried to think of the best way to get through this with minimal damage, and I saw only one choice: to answer the truth.

"You know the one who's good at math? I think she's pretty."

"Oh!" she exclaimed. "That's Hina. She's one-eighth German, you know. Huh, so that's your type. She's pretty, but I don't think she has a boyfriend or anything. If I were a guy, I might pick her, too. You've got good taste!"

"Egotistical much? Just because I agree with you doesn't mean I have good taste."

I took another drink. It was beginning to not taste so good.

On command, I drew another card. Nine more rounds, and it would be over. I didn't see myself getting out of this earlier than that, so I prayed I would get the high card from now on. But my luck didn't cooperate.

I drew the two of hearts, and she drew the six of diamonds.

She said, "The gods would favor the kind-hearted girl, after all."

"I think I might be an atheist now."

"Truth or dare?"

I thought for a moment, but my position remained the same as before. "Truth."

"If Hina is the cutest in our class, then what place am I? Just by looks."

I took a drink from my glass in search of liquid courage. She raised her own glass to her lips and took an even bigger drink than I had.

I said, "My answer is limited to the girls whose faces I remember, but you're number three."

"Wow. I know I asked, but now you've made me feel embarrassed. I didn't think you'd give me a straight answer."

"I just want to get this over with. So, no more fighting it. I give."

Her cheeks were bright red. It was probably the alcohol.

"Let's take our time, [Boy I'm Getting along With]-kun. We've got a long night ahead."

"That's a good point," I said. "Time does seem to stretch out when you're not having fun."

"*I'm* having a lot of fun," she said as she poured the plum liquor into both glasses. Since we'd run out of club soda, she filled them to the brim with the thick liquor. The smell had turned overly sweet, and the flavor even more so.

"Well, well," she said. "So, I'm third cutest, huh?" She gave me a boastful laugh.

"That's enough of that. I'm drawing again. Queen of diamonds."

"Don't you at least want to try to have some fun with this? I'll draw mine. Ah, the two of diamonds."

Seeing the look of disappointment on her face filled me with hope. My best defense in this game was to take as many turns from her as I could. I swore to myself once we were through these ten rounds, I would never again participate in whatever nonsense she claimed to be a game.

"Well," she said impatiently, "go on."

"Oh, right. Truth or dare?"

"Truth!"

"Okay, well then, ummm...."

I tried to think of something I wanted to know about her and found it right away. No other question even came close.

I said, "I've got one."

"Now I'm getting all nervous."

"What were you like as a child?"

She blinked. "Are you sure you want to go with that one? I was prepared to have to tell you my bra size or something like that."

"Shuddup," I said.

"Jerk!" she said.

She leaned back and looked upward, seemingly still enjoying herself. The point of my question wasn't to hear about some faintly remembered stories of her childhood. I wanted to know how a person ended up like her. As people grow up, we influence and are influenced by the people around us. What was the process that created my exact opposite?

As for why I wanted to know, I was simply fascinated. What kind of gap had existed between our life experiences to make us the kind of people we were? That question led to another, more troubling one: If I had taken one wrong step along the way, could I have ended up like her?

"Let's see... When I was a kid," she said. "I could never settle down."

"Yeah," I said. "I can easily imagine that."

"I know, right? You know how in grade school, the girls are taller than the boys? Well, I was the tallest in my class, and I'd get in fights with the boys. I'd break things, too. I was a problem child."

Maybe the size of a person's body affected the kind of person they became. I had always been small and physically weak, which could have been why I became introverted.

She asked, "Is that good enough?"

"Yeah," I said. "Let's do another."

After that, the gods did seem to favor the righteous, and I won the next five draws in a row. The cocky girl from the beginning of the game was gone now, and each time she lost, the girl and her pancreas forsaken by the gods drank and got more sullen—although, to be more precise, her mood didn't worsen when she lost as much as when I asked another question. By the time we had two rounds left, her face was deep red, her lips tightly puckered, and she seemed about to slide off the couch.

For the record, these were the five questions I asked, which prompted her to say, "What is this, an interview?"

Which hobby have you had the longest?

If I had to pick one, I guess I've always loved watching movies.

Which famous person do you most look up to, and why?

Sugihara Chiune! You know, the guy who gave visas to the Jews during World War II? I just think it's really cool that he persisted in doing what he thought was right.

What do you see as your strengths and weaknesses?

My strength is that I can get along with everyone. I have too many weaknesses, but I guess I'll say that I get distracted too easily.

What's made you the happiest in your life so far?

[laughs] Meeting you, I guess! [giggles]

Aside from your illness, what's been the hardest part of your life?

I think it was when my dog died when I was in junior high... What is this, an interview?

Managing a perfectly innocent expression, I said, "No, this is a game."

With tearful eyes, she howled, "Ask me something more fun!" Then she downed another glass and said, "Come on, drink."

She glared at me with enough danger in her eyes that I decided not to rankle her further, and I drank, too. The liquor had definitely gone to my head, but I was better at keeping a poker face.

"Two more rounds," I said, picking out a card and flipping it. "Jack of clubs."

"What?" she said, grumbling in a mix of profound sadness,

frustration, and irritation. "How can you have that much luck? Come on."

She flipped a card. I was confident I'd have the high card again, but when I saw her draw, a bead of sweat ran down my spine.

The king of spades.

"I... I did it!" She leaped to her feet with a cry of triumph, cut short when her legs didn't hold, and she toppled back down to the couch. Mood completely reversed, she chortled, amused by her own drunken state.

"Hey," she said. "Can I just give you the question and the command at the same time, and you can take your pick?"

"You've revealed yourself at last. It's gone from a dare to a command, has it?"

"Oh, right, right. Truth or dare, got it."

I said, "I suppose that's not against the rules."

"All right—truth or dare. Truth, say three things about me that you find charming. Dare, carry me to bed."

As quickly as she'd finished speaking, I started moving; it didn't take any thought. Even if I picked truth now, I'd still end up having to move her eventually. There was no reason to hesitate before choosing to get the job over with now. Besides, that question was heinous.

When I stood, my body felt lighter than it really was. I approached her on the couch. She giggled merrily. She was drunk, all right. I held my hand out in front of her to help her stand. She stopped laughing.

She asked, "What's that for?"

"I'm giving you my hand. Come on, stand up."

"I can't. My legs are jelly." Slowly, the corners of her mouth turned up. "Didn't you hear me? I said *carry* me."

I looked down at her.

"Should you carry me piggyback, maybe? Or sweep me up in your arms like—eek!"

Before she could embarrass me further, I put one arm behind her back and the other under her legs, then lifted her. I wasn't strong, but I had enough strength to carry her several steps, at least. I didn't allow myself to hesitate. This was going to be okay. I was drunk, and a minor indignity would be forgotten overnight.

Before she could manage any sort of reaction, I dumped the girl in my arms onto the bed. I could feel her warmth leaving my skin. Her expression was frozen in surprise. Between the alcohol and the exertion, I was a little winded, and I watched her as I caught my breath. Before long, her expression melted into a grin, and she began to giggle like a chirping bat.

"Now that was a surprise!" she said. "Thanks."

She sluggishly rolled over to the left side of the bed and faced the ceiling. For a moment, I hoped she might fall asleep like that, but then she began gleefully swatting at the bed with both arms while laughing some more. She didn't look at all ready to abandon the game.

I found my resolve and said, "All right, last round. I'll do you a favor and turn over your card for you. Tell me where you want me to draw from."

"Let's see. I want one from near my cup."

She settled down and let her arms flop casually to the bed.

Still standing, I turned over a card that was touching her nearly empty glass.

Seven of clubs.

"Seven," I said.

"Rishky," she said.

"Can I assume you mean risky?"

"Yeah, rishky."

She seemed to like the sound of her new word, as she kept repeating it out loud. I didn't let her distract me as I looked down at the ring of cards. Among them was my last. In a situation like this, some people would take their time to think and carefully make their choice, but they would be wrong. The cards were random; luck was the only element. It was better to act without pause. That way, there was less time to build up expectations—and disappointment.

Casually, I took a card from the pile. Trying not to let any thoughts break my concentration, I turned the card over.

Luck was everything.

It didn't matter how bravely I'd made my decision, that couldn't change a number.

My card was—

"Come on, what'd you get?" she asked.

"Six."

I was too honest and too clumsy a speaker to lie. Life might have been easier if I was the type of person who would flip over the board during a shogi match that wasn't going my way, but I didn't want to become that type of person, nor could I.

"Right on," she said. "Let's see, what should I go with?"

She went quiet. Feeling like a convict awaiting his execution, I stood and waited for her question.

A stillness, long absent, returned to the dimly lit room. This high up, almost no city noise filtered in from the outside, and no sounds spilled over from the adjacent rooms. An expensive hotel room could buy a lot of quiet. In my inebriated state, my breathing and heartbeat sounded loud in my ears. I could hear her steady breathing quite clearly, too. I wondered if she had fallen asleep, but when I looked, her eyes were open, staring at the dark ceiling.

Unable to bear standing in place any longer, I looked outside through a gap in the curtains. The bustling downtown was aglow with colorful, man-made light and showed no signs of sleeping.

"Truth or dare?" she said.

The silence broke without warning. I prayed that whatever she'd decided upon wouldn't be too harrowing. Without turning from the window, I answered, "Truth."

She took in a single deep breath and then asked that night's last question.

"If I..."

Her voice was soft, and her words caught. I waited.

"If I told you I was actually terrified of dying, what would you do?"

I turned to her.

Her voice had been so faint, I nearly got the chills. To avoid facing that feeling, I faced her instead. I needed to see if she was still alive.

I was sure she could feel my eyes on her, but her gaze remained fixated on the ceiling. Her lips were closed tight. She had no more to say.

Was that how she truly felt? I couldn't grasp her intention. I could have believed she was speaking the truth, but I also could have believed she was joking. If it was the truth, what was the right response? Even if it was a joke, what was the right response?

I didn't know.

The monster inside my chest started breathing again, and it laughed at my feeble lack of insight and perception.

As I stood there in fearful hesitation, my mouth opened, and the word came out of its own accord.

"Dare."

She said nothing at first. She didn't say if she approved or disapproved of my choice. Instead, still staring at the ceiling, she gave me her command.

"Sleep in bed with me. No arguing. No debate."

She began to sing, "Rishky, rishky."

I wasn't sure what was the right thing to do. But in the end, I couldn't flip over the shogi board.

I turned off the lights, got onto the other side of the bed with my back to her, and waited for sleep to take me away. Every now and then, she would change position, and I could feel the bed shift. We shared the bed, together but also separate, just as we were two people with our own thoughts and feelings; affecting each other, but still alone.

The bed was large enough for both of us to sleep on our backs with enough space in between.

We were innocent.

We were innocent and pure of heart.

I made the excuses, but no one forgave me.

We both woke at eight in the morning, to a cell phone ringing noisily. I got up and retrieved mine from my bag, but it was silent. I grabbed hers from the sofa where she'd left it the night before, and I handed it to her on the bed. The sleepy-eyed girl flipped the phone open and placed it to her ear.

I could hear the howls of the person on the other line even from where I stood.

"Sakuraaaaa! Where are you?"

The girl winced and held the phone away from her ear. Once the shouting subsided, she put it back and said, "Morning. What's up?"

"Don't give me that! I asked you a question. Where are you?"

Looking a little unsure, she stated, "Fukuoka." From the sound of things, her caller was appalled.

"What the hell is going on? Why did you lie to your parents and say you were on a trip with me?"

So, this was her best friend, then. She responded to the outburst with a carefree yawn and said, "How did you find out?"

"The PTA was passing along a message about something at school.

My parents are after yours on the phone chain, remember? When your mom called, I was the one who picked up. Explaining my way out of that one was a nightmare!"

"Sounds like you managed it though. Thanks, Kyōko, you're the best. How'd you do it?"

"I pretended to be my sister—but that's not the point! Why did you lie to your parents so you could go all the way to Fukuoka?"

"Well..."

"And if you really wanted to go that badly, you didn't have to make up that lie. We could have gone on a trip for real. You know I'd go with you."

"That sounds nice. Let's go on a trip together over summer break. When do your club activities go on break?"

"I'll check my calendar and let you know." I could hear the dry sarcasm in her friend's voice.

Our room was quiet enough that I'd been able to make out most of the conversation even when her friend wasn't shouting on the other end. I went to the sink, washed my face, and kept an ear listening while I brushed my teeth. The toothpaste here had a sharper taste than the one I used at home.

"What are you doing sneaking off all alone like you're some dying cat?"

I didn't find the unintended joke all that funny. My companion's reply was even less humorous, although it was true.

"I'm not alone."

She sent me an amused glance with eyes that were bloodshot

from last night's drinking. I wanted to sink my head into my hands, but one was occupied by my tooth brush, and the other by my water cup.

"You're... You're not alone? Wait. Who are you with? Is it your boyfriend?"

"No, come on. You know I broke up with him."

"Then who?"

"[Boy I'm Getting along With]-kun."

Stunned silence came from the other end of the phone. I was beyond caring at this point, and I kept brushing my teeth.

"You... Huh?" her friend sputtered.

"Listen to me, Kyōko."

The friend seemed to be listening.

Her voice became serious. "I know this doesn't make any sense to you, and it must seem very strange, but I promise I will explain it to you one day. I won't ask you to accept it, but please, forgive me. And I want you to keep this to yourself for now."

Her friend didn't seem to know how to respond. That only seemed natural. Why pass over your best friend to go traveling with a classmate you barely know?

The friend remained silent for a little while. The girl on the bed patiently held the phone against her ear. Finally, a voice came from the speaker.

"Okay."

"Thank you, Kyōko."

"That comes with conditions."

"Of course. Whatever you say."

"*Come home safe. Bring me back something tasty. And go on a trip with me over summer break. And one more thing—tell [Classmate with an Inexplicable Connection to My Best Friend] that if he does anything funny to you, I'll kill him.*"

She laughed and said, "Okay."

They exchanged a few words of goodbye and she hung up. I rinsed out my mouth and sat on the couch she'd stolen from me the night before. The cards were still scattered on the table, and I began picking them up. When I glanced at her, she was straightening her bed hair with her fingers.

I said, "It's nice you have a friend thinking of you."

"It really is," she said. "Oh, you may have heard, but apparently Kyōko is going to kill you."

"If I do anything funny to you, you mean," I reminded her. "When you tell her what happened, be sure to tell her I was a total gentleman."

"I seem to remember you carrying me to bed like a maiden in your arms."

"Oh, is that what you call it? I just felt like a mover hauling boxes."

"I'm pretty sure she'd kill you for thinking of it that way, too."

She took a shower to fix her hair while I waited. When she was done, we went down to the first floor for breakfast.

Breakfast was served as a lavish buffet that underscored just how high-class this hotel was. I made my breakfast a Japanese one by filling my plate with things like fish and boiled tofu. I returned to our window-side table, and when she came back, she was carrying a tray with a ridiculous amount of food.

"Breakfast is the most important meal of the day," she said, but she ended up leaving about a third of her food, which I ate. As I did, I advocated the merits of being a careful planner, like me.

Back in our room, I boiled some water. I made myself coffee, and she made herself tea. Sitting where we were the night before, we watched morning TV and relaxed for a bit. The room felt peaceful, with sunlight shining bright through the curtains. It seemed like we both had forgotten her final question of the night.

I asked, "What's the plan today?"

She sprang to her feet and sauntered to her sky blue backpack, from which she retrieved a notebook. She had our train tickets home tucked into its pages.

"Our train leaves at two-thirty," she said. "We'll have plenty of time to get lunch and find some gifts. Where should we go for the rest of the morning?"

"I don't know. I'll leave that to you."

We checked out in no hurry. The hotel staff bowed to us as we left.

She decided we would ride a bus to a well-known shopping mall. According to the guide book, the complex straddled a canal and featured everything from shopping to live theatre. Apparently, it had become a popular destination for foreign tourists. When we got there in person, the massive, bright red buildings were an impressive sight, and every bit the landmark.

We found ourselves in the central open air atrium, surrounded by grand, curving buildings, unsure of where to go. We wandered for a bit and happened upon a street performer dressed as a clown, who was performing in an open area beside the canal. We added ourselves to the audience.

The show, about twenty minutes long, was fun to watch, and afterward the clown made a comical display of asking for money. Like the high school kid I was, I put a hundred-yen coin in his hat. She happily put in a five-hundred-yen coin.

The girl said, "That was really fun. You should become a street performer, [Boy I'm Getting along With]-kun."

"Do you have any idea who you're talking to? I could never do a job that involves dealing with so many strangers like that. That was the most impressive part of the whole act."

"That's too bad," she said. "Maybe *I* should, then. Oh wait, I forgot, I'm going to die soon."

"Did you come up with this whole conversation just so you could say that? Look, you've got a year, right? Maybe you can't get to his level in that time, but if you practice, I bet you could get pretty good."

When she heard my advice, her face lit up with delight. It was the kind of smile that could make someone else happy, too.

"You're right!" she said. "Maybe I'll do just that."

Excited by her idea, she found a magic store in the mall and bought several kits for practicing. She didn't let me in the store with her. She explained she was going to perform the tricks for me one day, and picking them out with her would spoil it. Left behind, I stood in front of the store where a promo video featuring various magic tricks was playing. I watched the video alongside a group of grade school kids.

She came out with a shopping bag in hand and said, "And thus the legend was born—the magician who rose to sudden fame only to disappear as quickly as she came."

"Sure, maybe. But only if you're unbelievably talented."

"The way I figure it," she said, "one year to me is worth five to everyone else. It'll work out. Just you see."

I said, "I thought you said every day is worth the same value."

She seemed serious, her expression filled with even more strength and life than usual. Having a goal—even a short-lived one—made people light up. I wondered how much more conspicuous her radiance was with me standing next to her for comparison.

Time passed quickly as the radiant girl and I walked around the shopping center. She bought some clothes; when she found something that interested her, maybe a cheerful T-shirt or a skirt, she held them out to me and asked what I thought. I didn't know what was good or bad in women's fashion, so I responded with a noncommittal, "It suits you." Luckily, and mysteriously, that seemed to cheer her up. Since I wasn't lying, I didn't have to feel guilty.

At one point, we came across a store selling Ultraman goods. She bought me a vintage-style vinyl finger-puppet of a monster that looked like a dinosaur's skeleton. I didn't know why she'd chosen it for me, and when I asked, she said it suited me. I thought I'd get back at her by giving her an Ultraman one in return, but nothing I did could spoil her good mood.

With our hundred-yen plastic puppets on our fingers, we stopped to eat some ice cream before deciding to return to the train station.

We arrived exactly at noon. Seeing how we'd just had ice cream, we decided to hold off on lunch and instead shop for some local treats to bring home to her friend and her family. The train station had a large area filled with stalls dedicated to selling just such things. There was such a variety, she had trouble choosing.

She tasted several different samples before deciding on some candy and mentaiko—fish roe—for her family and another kind of candy for her friend. Since I was there, I bought myself a small box of pastries that had been awarded the Monde Selection gold medal several years running. I couldn't take a present home to my parents, as I had told them I was staying at my friend's house. I felt bad about it, but I didn't see any other option.

We then ate ramen for lunch at a different restaurant from the day before. Afterward, we still had time to kill, so we got some tea at a café before boarding the bullet train. The trip's end had me feeling fairly wistful, at least for me.

Unlike me, whose thoughts lingered on the past, she was already looking ahead.

"Let's go on another trip together," she said, gazing out the window beside her seat. "Maybe we'll do winter next."

I didn't know how to answer right away, but I decided the least I could do at this point was be cooperative.

"That could be nice."

"Look at you, all agreeable. Does that mean you had fun?"

"Yeah, this was fun."

It had been, too. I really meant it. My parents were always busy with work and took a hands-off approach to parenting, and

I didn't have any friends to travel with. This rare excursion had been a lot more fun than I'd expected.

She looked at me with surprise, but then her usual smile quickly returned, and she seized me by the arm. I didn't know what she was going to do, and I was frightened. Maybe she noticed my reaction, because she let me go, withdrawing her hand with an embarrassed, "Sorry."

"What were you going to do?" I asked, "Try to take my pancreas by force?"

"No, I was just happy you were being honest with me for once. Anyway, I had so much fun. Thank you for coming with me. I wonder where we should go next. I think I might want to go north. I want to experience the cold."

"Why would you torture yourself like that? I hate the cold. If our next trip is in the winter, I'd rather escape even farther south."

"Our outlooks *really* don't match up!"

While she puffed out her cheeks in mock displeasure, I opened the box containing my travel gift to myself. I shared one pastry with her and took a bite into another. The treat was round, buttery and cakelike, with a sweet bean filling.

When we arrived back in our hometown, the summer sky was beginning to take on a tinge of ultramarine. We changed over to a local train that took us to the station nearest our homes, and we rode our bikes together back to our school. Since we'd be seeing each other on Monday, our goodbyes were short before we went our separate ways.

When I got home, my parents were still out. I responsibly

washed my hands and rinsed out my mouth before heading to my room. I rolled onto my bed and felt suddenly tired. I was trying to figure out if it was because of exhaustion or a lack of sleep, or both, when I fell asleep.

My mom woke me up at dinnertime, and we watched TV as we ate yakisoba noodles. People say a trip ends when you get home, but I learned that wasn't true. My trip didn't end until I was eating dinner at home as usual. Normalcy had returned.

I didn't hear from her all weekend. Over those two days, I shut myself away in my bedroom to read as I always did. If I went out, it was alone, like to get an ice cream bar from the supermarket. Two days had passed without incident, when on Sunday night I realized something.

I was waiting to hear from her.

On Monday, when I got to school, everyone in class knew about our trip.

I found my school slippers in a trash can. I didn't know if that was related, but I could be sure I hadn't dropped them there myself.

Five

A SERIES OF UNUSUAL EVENTS began that morning. I
already mentioned my missing school slippers, but that was
just the start.

I arrived at school the same as always, and when I went to
retrieve my indoor slippers from the shoe rack, they were gone. I
was wondering what could have happened to them when someone said, "Morning..."

The girl was the only person in my class who ever greeted me,
but this didn't sound like her usual high-energy voice. Wondering
if her pancreas had gone kaput, I turned and was surprised to see
it wasn't her at all.

The best friend, standing at her shoe cubby, glared at me with
open hostility.

A shiver ran down my spine, but even an antisocial person
like me knew not responding would be rude. I returned her greeting with a noncommittal, "Morning." The friend stared me in the

eyes, then snorted and began exchanging her sneakers for school slippers. With my own pair missing, I didn't know what to do. For now, I kept standing there.

Once her slippers were on, I thought the friend would just go, but she gave me another dirty look and snorted again before she left. I didn't mind. That's not to say I enjoyed it—I'm not a masochist or anything—but I saw uncertainty in her eyes. I suspected she was having trouble deciding how to act toward me.

Even if she chose to be hostile, I respected her for greeting me. If our positions were reversed, I would have hidden around the corner until she was gone.

I gave the shoe racks a quick search but couldn't find my slippers. Hoping someone had taken them by mistake and would eventually return them, I decided to go to class in only my socks.

When I entered my classroom, I felt rude stares upon me from all sides, but I ignored them. When I decided to keep doing things with the girl, I had resigned myself to being scrutinized. She wasn't here yet.

I sat at my desk in the back row and transferred over what I needed for class from my school bag. Since this was the day we got our tests back and reviewed our answers, all I needed was the question sheet. I also put my pencil and a paperback into my desk.

I was glancing over last week's test questions and wondering what could have happened to my slippers when there was a commotion at the front of the classroom. I looked up to see the cause: The girl had strolled cheerfully into the classroom. A bunch of clamoring students rushed over to her, surrounding her in their circle. Absent among them was her best friend, who wore a conflicted expression as she watched from her desk. The friend glanced at me, and since I was looking at her, our eyes met before I quickly looked away.

I decided to stop paying any attention to the circle of students and their excited murmur. If the fuss had nothing to do with me, then I didn't care. If it did, then I didn't want to know.

I took the paperback from my desk and dove into the world within its pages. Chattering classmates were no match for a book-lover's powers of concentration.

At least that's what I thought, until I discovered that when one of those classmates was directly talking to me, the depth of my love for reading mattered not; I was going to be dragged back to the real world.

Now *two* people had talked to me in one day, and it was still morning. Another surprise. I looked up and saw the boy who had shown me his (previously unseen) potential as a cleaning partner. He looked down at me with a grin that, if I was being critical, I'd say showed no sign of a thinking mind beneath.

"Hey, [Controversial Classmate]," he said, drawing out the "a" at the end of my name. "Why'd you throw away your slippers, huh?"

I blinked a few times then said, "What?"

"I saw 'em in the restroom trash can. They still looked good to me, so why'd you toss 'em? Did you step in dog poop or something?"

I said, "I think dog poop in the school would be the bigger concern. But all right, thanks. I'd been upset because I'd lost them."

"Oh. Well you should be more careful. Do you want any gum?"

"No. Let me get my slippers. I'll be right back."

"Oh, hang on, did you go somewhere with Yamauchi? Everyone's talking about you again. You two really *are* dating, aren't you?"

Luckily, everyone who sat around me had gone to join the commotion, and they weren't around to hear this blunt and artless question.

"No," I said. "We just happened to meet at the train station. Someone must have seen us or something, I guess."

"Hmmm, okay. Well, if anything juicy happens, you tell me first."

Chomping on his gum, he went back to his seat. I could have dismissed him as naïve, but that seemed negative; he made the quality into a great virtue.

I got up from my desk and went to the nearest bathroom, where my slippers were indeed in the trash. Luckily, they were near the top, and nothing too unsanitary had been thrown away after to make them dirty, so I reclaimed them, dutifully slipped them on, and returned to class. When I entered the room, a brief silence fell before giving way to the chatter once more.

Class was uneventful. I got my tests back, and I'd done well enough. Toward the front rows, the girl and her friend were excitedly comparing their scores. The girl met my eyes once, and she proudly displayed the front sheet of her exams to me. I was too far back to make out the score, but I saw many more circles than strikes. The best friend noticed our exchange and looked uncomfortable, so I glanced away. That was the only contact the girl and I had that day.

We didn't speak the next day, either. My only interactions with my classmates were the best friend glaring at me again and that one guy offering me gum. The only other incident—and this was just a personal matter—was that I lost a pencil case I'd bought at a hundred-yen store.

The first opportunity to talk to her in several days came on the last day before our six-week summer break—although our class got the news we were to show up for two weeks of summer school, which made the distinction rather meaningless. Still, as the last day of the term, this was only supposed to be a half-day, ending after the assembly and announcements, but the librarian asked me to stay after to do some work. She asked me to bring the girl, as well.

On this rainy Wednesday, I initiated conversation with her in class for what may have been the first time. She was on chalk-board cleaning duty, and I walked to the front of class to inform her of our library work. I knew several classmates had their eyes on us, but I decided to ignore their stares. I didn't think she was bothered in the first place.

After class was dismissed, she had to stay behind to help close up our classroom. I went ahead to lunch in the cafeteria before continuing to the library. Few students were there, for this was the end of the term, after all.

Our job was to staff the counter while the librarian was at a teachers' meeting. During the meeting, I sat at the checkout desk reading a book. Two classmates came up separately with books to borrow. One was a timid girl who asked, "Where's Sakura?"

without showing any particular interest in me. The second was our class representative. He'd always come off as gentle-natured in class, and his tone and expression reinforced that impression as he asked, "Where's Yamauchi-san?" I responded to both the same, telling them she was probably still in our classroom.

She arrived not much later, bringing with her a smile that felt totally at odds with the gloomy weather.

"Yoo-hoo," she said. "Were you lonely without me?"

"'Yoo-hoo' yourself. Oh, a couple of our classmates were looking for you."

"Who?"

"I don't really remember their names. It was a timid girl and the class representative."

"Oh yeah," she said. "I know who you mean. Okay."

She flopped down onto a swiveling desk chair behind the counter, and the chair's metal parts creaked in protest, echoing throughout the quiet library.

I said, "I think you're hurting the poor thing."

"Is that something you should say to a young lady?"

"I don't think you're a lady."

She laughed mischievously. "Are you sure? You know, a boy told me he liked me yesterday."

"What?" I said. Her statement was so unexpected, I accidentally let my surprise show.

She lifted the corners of her mouth high; so high that creases formed between her eyebrows. It was thoroughly infuriating.

"He told me to meet him after class yesterday." She sighed

melodramatically. "That's when he confessed his innermost feelings to me."

"If that's true," I said, "I'm not sure he'd appreciate you telling me. It sounds personal."

"Well, I'm not going to tell you *who*. My lips are sealed—like Miffy."

She put her index fingers in the shape of an X in front of her lips.

"You mean Miffy the rabbit?" I said. "Are you one of those people who thinks the X is her mouth? Her face is divided in the middle—the top half is her nose, and the bottom half is her mouth."

I sketched the little cartoon rabbit for her. She exclaimed, "No way!" in total disregard to the quiet library, her eyes and mouth opened wide. The sight was satisfying. At last, I got my revenge for her insulting non-reaction to my trivia on Japanese dialects.

"I don't know what to say," she said. "I'm shocked. I feel like these last seventeen years have all been a lie. But anyway, this boy said he liked me."

"Oh, we're going back to that? So, what did you tell him?"

"I said I wasn't interested. Why do you think I did that?"

"Beats me," I said.

"I'm not going to tell you," she teased.

"Let me tell you something. If someone says, 'Beats me,' or 'Huh,' that means they're not interested enough to ask why. Have you never noticed that before?"

She looked ready with a comeback, but a student came up to check out a book and spoiled her timing.

After we processed the book—we were still doing our jobs, of course—she changed the subject.

"Since it's raining and we can't do anything fun outside today, you're coming over to my house instead."

"Nah. That's the opposite way from my house."

"You could at least come up with an interesting excuse. It's almost like you don't really want me to invite you over."

"Huh. It's almost like you really think I want to be invited over. I can't imagine what made you think that."

"What?" she said in mock outrage. "Ah, whatever. You talk like that, but you'll end up coming with me all the same."

She had a point. As long as she gave me some sort of solid justification, or threat, or the sense of a righteous duty, I would be swayed. If a path was presented to me, I wouldn't oppose it. That was simply because I was the boat of reeds; no other reason.

She said, "I haven't even told you the whole thing yet. When you hear what I've got, you might want to come over."

"My resolve is stronger than Fruiche. I'm not so sure you can break me."

"Fruiche? That's gloopier than anything. Man, Fruiche, huh? That brings me back. I haven't had any of that stuff in so long. I'll have to buy the mix next time I'm out. My mom used to make it for me when I was in grade school. My favorite is the strawberry one."

"Your train of thought is about as firm as yogurt. I bet you could mix that with my resolve."

"Maybe we should try."

She loosened the bow tie of her summer uniform and undid her top shirt button. She must have been having trouble with the heat. Or she was just being silly. Probably the latter.

She said, "Don't give me that look. Okay, back to the subject. So, you know how I told you before that I never read?"

"Yeah. Except for manga."

"Right. Well, later I realized that wasn't quite true. I *basically* never read books, but there's one book that I've loved since I was a little girl. My dad gave it to me. Now, tell me that doesn't interest you."

"I see. That actually does interest me. A person's favorite books reveals a lot about who they are. I'd like to know what kind of book someone like you likes. So, what's the book?"

She paused for dramatic effect, then said, "Have you ever heard of *The Little Prince?*"

"By Saint-Exupéry?"

"What?" she exclaimed. "You know it? Come on, that's a foreign book. I was sure even you wouldn't have heard of it. Darn it."

She pouted and slumped back in her chair, which let out another creaking wail.

I said, "If you don't know that *The Little Prince* is famous, you really must not be interested in books."

"It's famous? Then you've probably read it, too," she groaned.

"Actually, I'm a little embarrassed to admit I haven't yet."

"Really?"

She sprang up in her seat and leaned in to me. I scooted back along with my chair. She was grinning, of course. Apparently, I'd said something to make her happy—maybe a little too happy.

She said, "I mean, of course you haven't read it. I knew that all along."

"Don't you know people who tell lies get sent to hell?"

She ignored my remark. "If you haven't read it, you should. I'll let you borrow my copy. Come over to my house today and get it."

"Can't you just bring it to school?"

"You wouldn't want to make a frail young girl have to carry something so heavy, would you?"

"I'm going to take a wild guess and say it's a paperback. Isn't it?"

She offered, "I could bring it over to your house instead."

"What happened to the book being heavy?" I asked. "Ah, forget it. Arguing with you is as exhausting as it is pointless. Besides, if you'd go so far as to bring it to my house, I may as well spare you the trip and go to yours."

I'd file this one under righteous duty.

If I was to tell the truth, I was sure the school library would have a famous book like *The Little Prince,* but I didn't want to sour her good mood, so I didn't say anything. I didn't know why I hadn't yet read such a well-known story; it was probably just a matter of timing.

She said, "Well, well, when did you get to be so reasonable?"

"It's a little something I learned from you—a boat of reeds can't oppose a large ship."

"You know, every once in a while you say something that goes right over my head."

While I was eagerly explaining to her my use of metaphorical expression, the librarian returned. As had become our habit, the girl and I chatted with the teacher over tea and sweets. We told the librarian the unfortunate news that we had to come to school for the next two weeks for summer school, and then we left for the day.

Outside, thick clouds filled the sky and offered no hint of any sunlight to come. I didn't hate rainy days. Rain always seemed to close off the rest of the world, and on most days, that suited my mood rather than spoiling it.

"I hate rain," the girl groaned.

"Our outlooks really don't match, do they?"

"Does anybody seriously *like* rain?"

They do, actually. But I chose not to argue the matter and instead began walking ahead of her. I didn't know where exactly she lived, but her house was the opposite direction from mine, so I just turned the other way down the street in front of the school.

Catching up to walk beside me, she asked, "Have you ever been in a girl's room before?"

"I haven't," I replied, "but we're both high school students. I don't imagine it'll be all that shocking."

"I guess not. My room is pretty plain. Kyōko has all these band posters and things—her room is more like a guy's room than most guys' rooms are. That Hina girl you like, her room is all stuffed animals and cute things. Maybe the three of us should hang out together next time."

"No thanks," I said. "I can't talk in front of pretty girls—they make me too nervous."

"I know you're trying to suggest I'm not cute and I'm supposed to react to that and all, but it won't work. I haven't forgotten that you told me I was the third prettiest in class."

"Yeah, but what you don't know is I could only remember three girls' faces."

That was an exaggeration, although I really didn't remember the face of every girl in our class. The ability to remember faces wasn't all that useful to someone who didn't socialize much; maybe those mental muscles had atrophied through disuse. In any case, a competition shouldn't count when not all the contestants were present.

Her house ended up being almost exactly the same distance from the school as mine was. Tucked away in a neighborhood of single-family homes, her house had cream-colored siding and a red roof.

Since I was with her, I didn't need to hesitate before walking onto the property. A small fenced-in yard occupied the space between the street and her front door, so I didn't close my umbrella right away.

She ushered me in the front entrance and I fled inside like a cat from a wet place.

Raising her voice, she announced her arrival with a cheerful, *"Tadaima!"*

I hadn't met a classmate's parents since open house day in junior high, and I felt vaguely nervous. I said softly, "Um, hello. Sorry for intruding."

The girl said, "Nobody's home."

"If there's nobody here, then who were you greeting like that? There must be something wrong with your head."

"I was greeting the house. This is where I've grown up. The place is important to me."

Every now and then she could say something worthy of respect. I had no response. I told the house hello again and removed my shoes.

She went around turning on the lights, and life seemed to return to the house. She showed me to the washroom, where I washed my hands and rinsed out my mouth at the sink. Then we went to her bedroom on the second floor.

My first impression upon entering a girl's bedroom for the first time was: It was large. And by "it," I mean everything; the room itself, her television, her bed, her bookcase, her computer. For a moment, I became jealous, but then I realized the proportions were a manifestation of her parents' grief, and my envy dissipated.

"Sit wherever," she said. "If you need a rest, I'll even let you into my bed—but I will tell Kyōko."

She claimed the red task chair at her desk and began spinning around. I stood indecisively for a moment before sitting on her bed. The mattress was springy.

From my new vantage point, I surveyed her room again. Like she'd said, the style was typical. The room was much like my own, only differing in its size, the cuteness of the knickknacks, and the contents of our bookcases. Hers was filled only with manga, ranging from popular boys' comics to many I'd never heard of before.

She stopped spinning her chair and let out a nauseating belch. I was watching her with bored eyes when she suddenly looked up and said, "What should we play? Truth or dare?"

"I thought you were lending me a book. That's why I'm here, remember?"

"Relax," she said. "If you stay wound up like that you'll die before I will."

I gave her a dirty look, and she scowled back at me. I thought this might be a game where we would see which of us would get disgusted by the other first. If so, I was about to lose.

Casually, she stood and walked to her bookcase. I thought she might be getting *The Little Prince* for me, but instead she opened the lowest drawer and retrieved a folding shogi set.

"Let's play this," she said. "A friend left it here and hasn't come to get it back."

I didn't see any reason to say no, so I agreed. I won the match, but only after a drawn-out, ugly mess of a battle. I'd thought winning would be easy, but a competitive game against a real opponent was different than the shogi puzzles I played by myself, and I couldn't find my rhythm. When I finally had her king in check, she flipped over the board in frustration. Come on, now.

As I picked up the scattered shogi pieces from her bedspread, I looked out the window. The rain was still pouring.

Seeming to read my thoughts, she said, "You can go home when the rain lets up. Let's keep playing games until then."

She put away the shogi set, got out a video game console, and hooked it up to the front of her TV. I hadn't played any video games in a long time.

We started with a fighting game, one of those barbaric games where the players derive enjoyment from pressing buttons on the controller to make people on the TV hurt each other.

Since I didn't play video games that much, she gave me a little time to practice. I kept my eyes on the screen as I tried inputting some commands, and she gave me some helpful advice. But if I thought she was taking it easy on me, I'd misjudged her. When the time came for our match, she wiped the floor with my character, as if in revenge for our shogi game. She used special moves that changed the colors on the screen and made strange fireballs appear from her character's hands.

But I refused to go down without a fight. I gradually got the hang of the game, and soon I was able to dodge some of her attacks and throw her while she was guarding. When her character came charging across the screen in a reckless attack, I handily countered her. Just as I closed the gap between our win counts and was about to pull into the lead, she turned off the console. Come on.

I gave her a critical look, which she ignored. She was already inserting the next game, and she turned on the power switch.

She owned all sorts of games, and we played several against each other. The one that offered the best matchup was a racing game. The game had an element of competition, to be sure, but ultimately the battle was against time. From a certain perspective, my true opponent was myself. That aspect of racing seemed to fit my personality better than the other games.

We raced on her large-screen TV, and I would pass her go-kart, and she would pass mine. I wasn't talkative under normal circumstances; now that I focused on the race, I spoke even less. Meanwhile, she reacted loudly to almost everything. The total volume of sound in the world remained constant.

Sometimes she'd say something to try and break my focus, but as we entered the final lap of a race, she asked me a question that seemed only conversational.

"So, [Boy I'm Getting along With]-kun, do you ever think about getting a girlfriend?"

I evaded a banana peel on the race track and replied, "No, and I don't think I could anyway. I don't even have any friends."

"Then forget a girlfriend for now and start with making friends."

"I might if I feel like it."

"If you feel like it, huh?" she repeated. "Hey, can I ask you something?"

"What?"

"You definitely wouldn't want me as your girlfriend, right? Like, no matter what?"

The question was so outlandish—and so blunt, as her remarks often were—I reflexively looked away from the screen to her, and my go-kart veered and caused a spectacular wreck.

She laughed and said, "You crashed!"

I asked, "What are you talking about?"

"Oh, you mean about being your girlfriend? I was just checking. You don't have a thing for me, right? You don't want to date me, like, no way... Right?"

I was quiet for a moment, then said, "I don't."

"Good," she said. "That's a relief."

A relief? I didn't understand why she should feel relieved. I tried to think it through.

Did she really suspect that I had romantic intentions?

Was she fearful that I'd gotten the wrong idea after sharing a hotel room with her and coming up to her room?

I hadn't done anything to deserve such suspicion.

I was uncomfortable. It wasn't a feeling I was accustomed to. An unpleasant knot began forming in the pit of my stomach.

I finished the race and let go of the controller.

The feeling took hold deep inside and lingered there. I wanted to escape before she noticed something was wrong.

"All right, I'll take that book now," I said. "I'm going home."

I stood and walked to her bookcase. The rain was every bit as strong as before.

"Aw, you can stay longer," she said. "But fine. Hold on."

She came over to her bookcase and stood behind me. I could hear her breathing; it sounded heavier than normal.

Whatever her deal was, I looked for the book on her shelves, starting from the top and moving down. Maybe she was looking for it, too. That made me a little annoyed—if she was planning on lending me the book, she should have just left it where she could find it.

I heard her let out a deep breath, and I saw an arm reaching past me into my field of view. I figured she had spotted the book first, but then her other arm had also appeared on my other side.

Suddenly, I lost balance.

I'd had so little experience with people making physical contact with me, and at first, I couldn't comprehend what was happening.

The next thing I knew, my back was pressed against the wall beside the bookcase. My left hand was free, but my right hand was pinned to the wall just above shoulder height. Her breathing was closer, and I could feel her heartbeat; her warmth, a sweet fragrance. Her right arm pressed against the top of my chest. I couldn't see her face, and her mouth was at my ear. Our cheeks were close enough to touch, and every now and then, they did.

What are you doing? I moved my lips to ask, but I couldn't make my voice come out.

She whispered, "Do you remember I told you I made a list of things I wanted to do before I die?"

I could feel her breath on my ears. She didn't wait for me to reply.

"The reason I needed to ask you if you wanted me for your girlfriend was so I can do something on that list."

Her black hair swayed before my eyes.

"It's also why I invited you over."

I thought I heard a tiny laugh.

"Thank you for telling me you didn't. It was a relief. If you said you did, I wouldn't be able to cross this off."

I couldn't understand what she was saying, or what was happening.

"What I want to do is..."

She smelled sweet.

"...something I'm not supposed to do with someone who isn't my boyfriend."

Something she's not supposed to do? *Something she's not supposed to do?*

Her words echoed in my head. What did she mean? Was she talking about what she was doing right now? Something she was about to do? Everything we'd done in the past? All three could be true. Nothing we had done was what we were supposed to do. I wasn't supposed know about her illness. She wasn't supposed to be spending the rest of her short life with a boy she didn't like. Sharing a hotel room, me being in her bedroom—everything was something we weren't supposed to be doing.

"This is a hug," she said, apparently reading my thoughts. We were close enough to feel each other's heartbeats. Maybe mine told her what I was feeling. Hers didn't tell me the same. "What I'm not supposed to do is what's next."

I didn't know how to act.

"With you, [???]-kun..."

I didn't say anything.

"I can do something wrong."

I had no clue how I should respond, but I used my free hand to remove her arm from my chest. I moved her to arm's length, so I no longer felt her breathing and her heartbeat. But now I could see her face. Her cheeks were flushed deep red, and this time, she hadn't been drinking.

When she saw my face, she looked surprised. I was shaking my head weakly, even if I didn't know what I was rejecting.

Our eyes met. Silence clung to us.

I watched her expression. Her eyes darted back and forth before settling somewhere off to my side. Then the corners of her mouth slowly lifted, as if she were trying not to smile, and she looked at me.

Then she started laughing—first a snicker, unable to be contained, followed by a full-on roaring laugh. I didn't join in.

"As if!" she said. She released my right arm, brushed away my hand, and kept on laughing.

"Oh my God, I'm so embarrassed. That was a joke. A joke! Another prank. Don't be so serious. You made me feel embarrassed."

Her outburst left me dumbfounded.

She was still talking. "That took a lot of courage. To just throw myself at you like that, I mean. But a prank needs to be grounded in reality, you know? Yep, that took guts for me. And when you didn't say anything, it was like you thought it was real. Did you get nervous? I'm glad I made sure you weren't interested in me—otherwise that could have gotten *too* real just now! Well, I pulled it off anyhow. The prank only worked because it was you. Oh, what a thrill that was."

For the first time since meeting her, I felt true anger at her. I didn't understand why this was what finally triggered that reaction, but it had.

The girl was still talking, as if to chase away the embarrassment she'd brought upon herself. The rage I felt slowly took form inside me, until it was more than could be melted away on its own.

Who did she think I was? I felt like she was making a mockery of me. Maybe she was.

If this was what associating with other people was like, then I had been right to never want to socialize with anyone. They could all get a pancreatic disease and die for all I cared. Then I had an even better idea: I would eat all their pancreases. I was the only righteous one.

I put my hands on her shoulders and pushed her onto the bed.

She shouted, but I didn't hear. Anger had blocked all sound from my ears.

I pressed her upper body to the bed, then let go of her shoulders and grabbed her arms, holding her there. My mind was blank. I wasn't thinking anything.

When she realized what had happened, she wriggled a little bit to try and get free, but she soon gave up and looked up at my face, now casting its shadow upon her. I still didn't know what my expression must have looked like.

Sounding confused, she said, "[Boy I'm Getting along With]-kun? What are you doing? Let go. You're hurting me."

I said nothing. I just looked her in the eyes.

"That was just a little joke," she said. "I was only playing around, like I always do."

I didn't know what would satisfy my anger. I couldn't comprehend myself.

While I remained mute, her expressive face went through a range of emotions she'd learned to display over a lifetime of social interactions.

She grinned. "Ah ha," she said, "you've decided to play along with my joke. You're a good sport. All right, that's enough now, let me go."

She started to look worried. "Come on, what's wrong? This isn't like you, [Boy I'm Getting along With]-kun. You don't play tricks on people. Right? Let me go."

She got angry. "Enough is enough! Do you think you can do this to a girl? Let me go now!"

I kept staring at her, my eyes as dispassionate as I could make them. She didn't look away. As we gazed into each other's eyes atop the bed, the scene was almost dreamlike.

Finally, she stopped saying anything. The loud rain outside her window sounded like condemnation. I could hear her breathing—I could even hear her blinks—and they seemed to be questioning me.

I kept staring at her, and she kept looking at me.

And then I saw it.

She had gone silent, her expression still, and tears had welled in her eyes.

As soon as I saw them, my anger vanished like it had never been there. I didn't know where the emotion went; I didn't even know where it came from.

In place of that bitter feeling came a growing regret.

Gently—as if that mattered now—I released her arms and stood. She looked up at me, bewildered. I don't know how she looked after that, because I couldn't bear to look at her again.

"Sorry," I said. She didn't answer. She remained on the bed, just as I'd pinned her there.

I picked up my things from the floor where I'd left them, then put my hand on the doorknob to escape.

"[Cruel Classmate]-kun..."

Hearing her voice from behind, I froze for a moment then replied with my back to her.

"I'm sorry. I'm going home."

I opened the door to her bedroom, which I'd probably never see again. Walking quickly, I fled. Nobody chased after me.

Out in the rain, I took a few steps before realizing my hair was getting soaked. I calmly opened my umbrella before walking into the street. The scent of summer rain drifted up from the asphalt.

As I traced my path back to the school, I scolded the part of me that wanted to look over my shoulder. The rain was getting stronger, pouring now.

Now that my head had cooled, I thought about what had happened.

But no matter how long I thought, the only answer I found was regret and total disappointment in myself. What had I done?

I didn't know that directing my anger at another person could hurt them so badly. I didn't know it could hurt me so badly.

Did you see her face? I scolded myself. *Did you see her tears? That was her hurt pouring out.*

My teeth ached, and I realized I'd been grinding them. I never thought the day would come when I inflicted physical pain on myself because of a relationship. I was going crazy. But I wasn't so deluded as to consider this pain a penance. Pain wouldn't absolve me of my crime.

Her prank was what made me angry; her joke had rubbed me the wrong way. That was the truth, but even so, that didn't excuse the use of violence against her. It didn't matter if she hurt me, whether or not she intended to.

Did she hurt me? I asked myself. *How? What got hurt?*

I recalled her smell and her heartbeat, but I didn't know what those memories meant. All I knew was her insult was something I couldn't let go. Acting out of irrational emotion, I had hurt her.

I walked the street lined with large detached homes. It was a weekday afternoon, and no one else was around.

If I was to suddenly disappear, no one would notice.

The quiet and the stillness of the street made the calm male voice calling my name from behind all the more startling.

"[Uninteresting Classmate]-kun."

I turned around to see a classmate holding an umbrella. Until he spoke to me, I hadn't noticed his presence at all. Two things puzzled me: One, that he talked to me; two, he had an intense expression, instead of the agreeable smile I thought of him as always wearing. He looked almost angry.

This was the second time we'd spoken in the same day. That rarely happened with anyone.

He was our class representative, and he always came off as cool-headed and genuine. Normally, he had no reason to interact with me, and I was curious why he did so now. I was still shaken from before, but I composed myself and said, "Hey."

He just stared at me in silence. Seeing nothing to do but try again, I said, "So you live around here, huh?"

After a moment, he said, "No, I don't."

He was definitely in a bad mood. Maybe he hated the rain, too. The rain always meant the annoyance of having to carry more things around. Although right now he just had on his street clothes and was only carrying an umbrella.

I looked at his face. Lately, I was beginning to be able to perceive people's emotional state from the look in their eyes. Hoping to find some clue as to why he would talk to me, even if doing so seemed to displease him, I met his stare.

I didn't say anything else. I was juggling the efforts of inspecting his expression while keeping my own emotions in check, and he lost patience first. He gritted his teeth and spat my name as if it was a bitter-tasting bug in his mouth.

"What about you, [Uninteresting Classmate]? What are you doing around here?"

I wasn't particularly bothered that he left off the "-kun" this time. What stuck with me was that he didn't sound like he was calling me [Uninteresting Classmate]. How he said my name came off more like [Unforgivable Person], or something like that. I didn't understand why he would think that, but I decided to go with it until I knew more.

When I didn't respond, he sneered and said, "What's the matter, [Unforgivable Person], didn't you hear me? I asked you what you're doing here."

"I had an errand."

"It's Sakura, isn't it?"

Hearing that familiar name, my chest tightened. My breath

caught in my throat, and I couldn't speak right away. He wasn't in the mood for waiting.

He repeated, "I said, it's Sakura, isn't it?"

I stayed mute.

"Say something!"

Grasping at some faint hope that he was mistaken, I said, "If by Sakura, you mean the girl in our class, then yes."

He clenched his teeth, and in that moment, I knew beyond any doubt that his animosity was directed at me. I just didn't know why he felt that way.

I tried to think it through, but quickly found the answer from the next thing he said.

"Why would Sakura," he said, interrupted by his own heavy breathing. I waited. "Why would Sakura be with someone like you?"

Oh. I get it.

I almost spoke my revelation aloud but consciously decided not to. Now I knew what he felt. I scratched my head, uncomfortable. This was going to be tedious.

If only he'd stop and listen, I could talk my way around this in any number of ways, or possibly given him a proper explanation, but his misdirected anger had deprived him of reason.

I considered the possibility that we hadn't run into each other today by accident. I could conceive countless scenarios; for instance, maybe he had tailed us from school.

He was probably in love with her. And now he was wrongly jealous of me. He'd lost the ability to observe with objectivity; he'd lost perspective. What else had he lost?

I decided to start with the tactic I saw as mostly likely to succeed: explaining the truth.

I said, "Our relationship isn't what you think it is."

Rage filled his eyes. *This isn't going well,* I thought, but before I could say anything else, he pressed me further, this time his voice combative and loud, drowning out the rain.

"Then you tell me what the hell it is! You're eating together, just the two of you, going on vacation, and today you went to her house *alone.* The whole class is talking about you. You've started clinging to her, out of nowhere."

I was a little curious how word of our trip had gotten out.

I explained, "I wouldn't say I'm clinging to her. I guess I'm not sure what I'd call it. If I said I was letting her go out with me, that would be too arrogant, but if I said she was letting me go out with her, that wouldn't be giving myself enough credit."

Noticing he had winced both times I said we were going out, I quickly clarified, "When I say we're going out together, I don't mean, like, going out *going out.* We're not *dating.*" I shook my head. "In any case, what's going on with me and her isn't what you or the rest of our class thinks it is."

"She's spending time with you."

After a moment, I said, "That's right."

His words dripped with hate. "With someone as sullen and antisocial as you."

I didn't have an argument there. I assumed that was how I came off, and maybe that was how I really was.

If he wanted to know why she would choose to spend her

time with me, well, so did I. She'd told me I was the only person who could give her normalcy and reality. I believed her, but somehow that answer seemed insufficient.

I kept quiet. He glared at me intensely, but his expression remained frozen, and he just stood there in the rain.

The silence stretched long. So long, in fact, I thought our conversation must have been over. Maybe he had realized his rage was baseless, and he was overcome with regret just as I had been. Or maybe he hadn't. Maybe he was still too angry to think.

I didn't care which was true. Either way, neither of us had anything left to gain here. I thought if I turned my back and walked away, he'd just watch me go, so that's what I did. Or maybe I simply wanted to be alone again as quickly as possible. I didn't care which was true, my actions would have been the same.

If I'd truly stopped to think, I would have realized my only experience with people blinded by love were characters in my books. It was presumptuous to try and predict the actions of a living, breathing human being when I'd never had a true emotional connection with one before. Characters in a story weren't like people in real life. Stories weren't reality. Reality wasn't as pretty.

I keenly felt his glare on my back as I walked away, but I didn't turn to look. No one would have gained anything from that. I hoped that, by keeping my back to him, I would communicate how far-fetched it was that the girl could possibly be in love with someone who thought of human relationships as mathematical equations. The message probably didn't get through.

I didn't understand love wasn't the only thing that could impair a man's judgment; so could logic. Consequently, I didn't realize he had followed me until his hand grabbed my shoulder.

"Wait!" he said.

I stopped and turned to look at him. Misunderstanding or not, I was getting tired of his attitude. I kept the annoyance from my expression.

"I'm not finished talking to you!" he said.

Maybe I was getting worked up, too. I'd never been in an altercation before—one person's emotions butting against another's. Looking back, I think in that moment, I had lost my capacity for rational thought.

Words came from my mouth with clearly no other purpose but to hurt him.

"Let me clue you in on something. It might do you some good." I stared him in the eye and spoke with the intent of gutting him. "She hates clingy guys. I guess her previous boyfriend was that way."

His expression contorted into something uglier than his earlier scowl. I didn't know what the expression meant, but I didn't care. Knowing wouldn't have changed the outcome.

A strong impact struck me somewhere around my left eye. I stumbled backward, then fell butt-first onto the wet asphalt. The rain immediately seeped into my school uniform. My open umbrella clattered stupidly to the ground and rolled there. My school bag fell, too. With surprise and incomprehension, I looked up at him. I could barely see out of my left eye, the vision blurred.

Even though I didn't know exactly what had happened, I understood I'd been the recipient of some sort of violence. A person doesn't simply fall over of his own accord.

He shouted, "What do you mean, 'clingy'? I... I..."

He was facing me, but I could plainly tell his words weren't directed to me. I had incurred the wrath of a more powerful force. I had tried to hurt him but got hurt myself. I felt ashamed and deeply regretted what I had done.

This was my first time being punched, and it sure did hurt. I knew why I felt pain where he'd hit me, but I didn't understand why I hurt on the inside, too. If the day kept going like this, I thought my heart might break.

Still sitting on the wet pavement, I looked up at him. My left eye still hadn't recovered its vision.

Breathing heavily through his nose, this boy—who I guessed was probably her ex-boyfriend, although I didn't know for sure at the time—looked down at me and said, "Someone like you has no right getting close to Sakura!"

He took something from his pocket and threw it at me. I uncrumpled the object and saw it was the bookmark I had lost. Now I could connect the dots.

"It was you," I said.

He didn't answer.

I had believed his handsome features were a reflection of his gentle nature. When he was guiding discussions at the front of the class, when he occasionally came to the library to borrow books, he had done so with an easygoing smile. But I'd only seen the image he carefully portrayed to the outside world, not what was in his heart. She had been right: What was real on the inside mattered, not appearances.

I thought about what I should do. I had hurt him first; calling his reaction self-defense wasn't that much of a stretch. Sure, he may have gone a bit too far, but I couldn't know how deeply I'd hurt him, so getting to my feet and punching him back didn't seem appropriate.

Standing above me, he still seemed incensed. I needed to calm him down but saying the wrong thing to him—or maybe even the *right* thing—may just throw more fuel onto the fire. I was the one who had pushed him over the edge already.

As we stared at each other, I began thinking he was more in the right than I was. He must have truly liked her. Maybe his methods were a little clumsy—or rather, they were the cause of his troubles—but he was honest about his feelings toward her, and he wanted to spend his time with her.

That's why he hated me: for stealing time they could have spent together.

And what of me? If I had never learned she would be dead in a year, I never would have gone out to eat with her, traveled with her, or spoiled things between us at her house. Her death connected us, but death awaited everyone. What else had brought us together but random chance? We had been spending time together because of a fluke. He wanted to be with her out of genuine intent and emotion. I had no such claim.

Even with my social inexperience, I understood one basic

truth: The one who was in the wrong must yield to the one who was in the right.

Okay, then. I would let him beat me until he was satisfied. It was my fault for trying to have a relationship with someone without understanding how other people's feelings worked.

I met his glaring eyes in an attempt to signal, *I yield*. But the message didn't get through.

A figure appeared, standing behind the heavily breathing boy. The girl said, "What...is going on?"

He turned as if struck by lightning. His umbrella jostled and sent raindrops spilling onto his shoulders. I watched them as if I was a spectator, unsure if her arrival was good timing or bad.

Holding her umbrella, she looked back and forth between the class representative and me as she tried to piece together what was going on.

He looked about to say something, but before he could, she ran over to me. She picked up my umbrella and offered it.

She said, "[Cruel Classmate]-kun, you'll catch a cold like that."

I accepted her gesture of kindness, although I felt unworthy. Then she gasped.

"[Cruel Classmate]-kun! You're bleeding."

Looking upset, she took a handkerchief from her pocket and held it against my left brow. I hadn't realized I was bleeding. I'd thought he'd struck me with his bare hands. *Had he used a weapon?* I wondered, although in that moment, I wasn't interested in the details.

Instead, I looked at his face. He was still standing in the

same place as before, having been passed by as she ran over to me. Words couldn't describe how drastically his expression had changed. I'd read the description "overflowing with emotion" before, and now I'd seen firsthand what those words meant.

She was saying, "What happened to you?" and, "Why are you bleeding?" and so on. I was ignoring her, not intentionally, but because his expression had completely captured my attention. He answered her for me.

"Sakura..." he said. "What are you doing with someone like that?"

Keeping her handkerchief pressed against my brow, she looked over her shoulder at him. When he saw her face, he grimaced again.

She said, "Someone like that...? You mean [Cruel Classmate]-kun?"

"Yeah, him," he said, his tone defensive. "He's been hanging on to you, so I took care of him. He won't be bothering you anymore."

Maybe he believed she'd think better of him now. Maybe he wanted to her to notice him again. But he couldn't see what she was thinking.

I had now completely taken on the role of observer, and all I could do was watch the scene unfold. She had frozen, her gaze on him with one arm raised to keep the handkerchief on my forehead. He had on a half-smile, like a child awaiting his praise. The other half was scared.

A few seconds later, the fear took over the rest of his face.

Finally, she spoke a single word, as if all her emotions had coalesced into a ball in her gut that needed spitting out.

"Creep."

He looked dumbstruck.

She immediately turned to me, and her face took me by surprise. I'd thought she possessed a wide range of emotions, but that they all held at least an element of cheerfulness. Even when she was angry, even when she cried, her expression was never dark. I had been wrong.

This was a look I hadn't seen from her before. It was a look intended to wound.

When she looked back at me, her expression quickly transformed into a smile mixed with uncertainty. She helped me to my feet. My pants and shirt were soaked through, but at least this was still summer, and I wasn't cold. The summer air kept me warm, as did her hand on my arm.

I picked up my bag. She pulled me along as she walked in the boy's direction. I looked at his face; seeing him so crestfallen, I didn't think he'd be stealing any of my belongings anymore.

We walked past him, and I thought she'd keep propelling me forward, so when she suddenly stopped, I nearly collided into her back. Our umbrellas knocked into each other and sent fat water drops falling.

Without turning, she spoke in a voice that was somehow simultaneously quiet and loud.

"I don't like you anymore, Takahiro. Don't ever do anything else to me or anyone around me again."

The boy she'd called Takahiro said nothing. I looked at him one last time; he was facing away from us now. He seemed to be crying.

She dragged me all the way back to her house. We went inside but didn't speak, aside from her handing me a towel and a change of clothes and telling me to take a shower. I did just that.

Until I'd borrowed the clothing—a men's T-shirt, boxer shorts, and track pants—I hadn't known she had a brother several years older than her. I didn't even know who was in her family.

After I changed clothes, she called me into her bedroom. She was sitting formally on her floor.

It was there that we did something I'd never done before. As I rarely associated with others, I didn't know what to call two people trying to speak openly and honestly with each other.

She called the process "making up."

Of all the human interactions I'd experienced before this point, this was the one that most made me itch with embarrassment.

She apologized to me. I apologized to her. She explained that when she hugged me, she thought I would look uncomfortable but then laugh. So I explained that for a reason I didn't understand, I felt like she was making a fool of me, and I got angry. She said she came after me in the rain because she didn't want to let things stay bad between us, and she had cried when I pushed her over purely because she was afraid of a man's physical strength.

I apologized from the bottom of my heart.

During our talk, I brought up the boy we'd left in the rain because I was still curious about him. My conjecture proved correct: The class representative had been her most recent boyfriend. I told her what I had thought as the rain poured onto me—that she was better off with somebody who had genuine feelings for her. We had only encountered each other in the hospital by pure chance.

As soon as I said that, she admonished, "You're wrong. It wasn't chance. Everyone is where they are because of the choices they've made. Our choices led us to being in the same class. Our choices brought us to the hospital. Not chance. There's no such thing as fate. All the choices you've made and all the choices I've made brought us together. You and I met by our own decisions."

I was silent. There was nothing I could say. I was amazed at how much I learned from her. If she had more than a year left to live—if she could somehow live longer—how much more could she teach me, after everything I'd already learned? I was certain that no amount of time would have been enough.

I borrowed a plastic bag for my wet clothes, along with the fresh clothes on my back and the book she'd promised me. I informed her that I read my books in the order in which I obtained them, and a number were ahead on the queue. She told me I could just return the book to her in a year, and I agreed. In not so many words, I made the promise that we would keep getting along as long as she lived.

The next day, I returned to school for the first day of summer school. My slippers were where they were supposed to be.

When I went to class, she wasn't there. When first period started, she still hadn't come. Nor was she there the next hour, or the one after that. Even after the school day was over, I hadn't seen her.

That night, I learned why.

She had been hospitalized.

Six

I DIDN'T SEE HER UNTIL the Saturday of that week in her
hospital room. It was morning, and the clouds were keeping
the heat at bay. She'd texted me the hospital's visiting hours, and
I left to see her—although to say I *went* wouldn't quite be right;
rather, I had been summoned.

She had a private room. When I arrived, no one else was visiting her, and she was standing by her window, facing outside. She
wore a standard hospital pajama set and had a tube hanging from
her arm, and she was performing a bizarre dance. I called to her
from behind, and she made a startled little jump, then fled shriek-
ing to her bed and burrowed herself under the blankets. I sat on a
folding chair beside her bed and waited for her to calm down. All
at once, she became quiet and sat up as if nothing had happened.
Her mercurial nature wasn't bound by time or place.

She said, "You can't just show up without warning me like
that. I thought I'd die of embarrassment."

"If you managed to be the first person in history to die that way, at least I'd have a funny story to tell for the rest of my life. Here, I brought you a present."

"What?" she exclaimed. "You didn't have to. Oh, strawberries! Let's eat them together. There are plates and stuff in that cabinet over there. Why don't you grab what we need?"

As asked, I retrieved a knife and a pair of plates and forks from a white cabinet against the wall and returned to the bedside folding chair. I'd bought the strawberries with money my mom gave me when I told her I'd be visiting a classmate in the hospital.

I cut the stems from the strawberries and began eating as I asked her how she was doing.

She said, "I'm completely fine. Some of my numbers were a little off, and my parents got all worked up and put me in the hospital, but it's nothing. I'll be in here for a couple weeks while they pump me full of some special medicine, and then I'll be back in school."

"Our extra classes will be pretty much over by then. We'll be on summer break for real."

"Oh, right. You and I will have to make some plans, then."

My eyes followed the tube from her arm to a metal pole on casters with a hanging pouch filled with clear liquid. A question came to me, and I asked it.

"What are you telling everyone—like your best friend, Kyōko-san?"

"I'm telling them I'm having my appendix removed. The hospital staff are going along with the story. Now that I've seen how worried my friends are about me, it's even harder to imagine telling them the truth. But I don't know, maybe I should ask the guy who pushed me onto my bed a few days ago what to do. So, what do you think, [Boy I'm Getting along With]-kun?"

"I think you should at least come clean with Best Friend-san—I mean Kyōko-san, but then again, I guess I should trust the decision of the girl who threw her arms around me a few days ago."

"Don't remind me! You're making me embarrassed again. I'm going to tell Kyōko you pushed me over. I don't want you to cause any trouble when she comes to kill you."

"You'd make your best friend a killer? That's twisted."

She made a face at me and shrugged. She was the same as always.

She'd told me she was fine over text, but I was relieved to see her acting as lively as ever. I'd feared her illness had progressed faster than expected and that she'd run out of time. But as far as I could tell from looking at her, that wasn't the case. Her expression was bright, and she moved with energy.

Feeling reassured, I opened my school bag and took out a brand-new notebook.

"Now that we've had our snack," I said, "it's time to study."

"What? C'mon, can't we just sit around a while first?"

"I came here because you asked me to help you study. Besides, all you've been doing here is sitting around."

I had a proper justification to come visit, beyond just seeing her. She'd asked me to take notes for her in class over the past several days then catch her up on the review lessons she'd missed.

When I promptly replied that I would, she acted surprised that I was being so agreeable. How rude.

I handed her the blank notebook and a pen and gave her a summary of the summer school classes, shortening the lessons by cutting out the parts I didn't think she needed to bother learning. For her part, she listened attentively. Including breaks, my mock class was over in about an hour and a half.

"Thanks," she said. "You know, [Boy I'm Getting along With]-kun, you're great at teaching. You should become a teacher."

"No thanks. Why do you keep suggesting jobs for me where I have to deal with other people?"

"Maybe I just want you to do the things I would be doing if I didn't have to die."

"Don't say that. That makes me the bad guy every time I reject your suggestions."

She giggled and placed the notebook on a brown shelf beside her bed, where magazines and manga stood in a row. Being hospitalized must have been tremendously boring for such an active person. The boredom may even drive her to perform bizarre dances.

The time was just before noon. She'd told me her best friend was coming in the afternoon, and I had already decided I'd leave before then. When I told her as much, she said, "Aw, you could stay and join in our girl talk," but I politely declined. I'd worked up an appetite playing at being a teacher, and I'd already accomplished what I'd set out to do for the day, which was to make sure she was all right.

"Before you go," she said, "let me show you a magic trick."

"You learned one already?"

"Just a basic one. I've got others I'm already practicing, though."

She'd chosen a card trick—one of those where I pick a card and she names it without looking. For how little time she'd had to practice, she was good at it. Having never studied magic myself, I wasn't able to figure out how the trick worked.

She said, "I'll do something tougher next time, so look forward to it."

"I will look forward to it. Maybe your last act will be escaping from a box that's on fire."

"Like escaping from the crematorium? I won't be pulling that one off."

"Yes, that was the joke."

"Sakuraaa," called a cheerful voice from the doorway. Reflexively, I looked over my shoulder. "How are you—oh. You again."

The best friend had come striding into the hospital room, but when she noticed me, she halted and scowled. She seemed to be getting more openly hostile toward me. If things kept going as they were, I didn't see how I would fulfill the girl's request that I get along with her best friend after her death.

I rose from the chair, said a quick goodbye, and began leaving. The best friend was glaring at me, and I made an effort to avoid her gaze. I'd watched a nature program last night that said to never look a wild animal in the eyes.

Just when I was feeling optimistic that I'd be able to sneak out without any mutual interference between me and the beast, the girl on the bed remembered something outrageous and said it.

"[Boy I'm Getting along With]-kun," she called to me. "That reminds me, did you bring my brother's boxers and pants—you know, the ones I let you borrow?"

I had never cursed my carelessness as much as I did in that moment. I had brought her brother's clothes in my bag with the intention of returning them.

But there was nothing I could possibly say now.

I turned around to see her grinning. Her friend beside her looked aghast. I did my best to appear composed as I took the plastic bag containing the clothes from my school bag and handed them to her.

"Thanks," she said. Still grinning devilishly, she looked back and forth between me and her friend.

Just once, I glanced at the friend, perhaps out of some foolish impulse—the primitive desire to look at something terrifying. The friend had already gotten rid of the astonished look, replacing it with a glare that could kill. Maybe I was imagining things, but I thought I heard her growling like a lion.

I immediately looked away from the best friend and scurried out of the room. Just before I crossed the doorway, I heard the friend beginning her interrogation with a harshly whispered, *"Boxers?"*

Not wanting to get embroiled in any further trouble, I quickened my pace.

—— ✳ ——

When the next week came, and I went to school on Monday as I was supposed to, a ludicrous rumor about me was running rampant throughout the class.

My classmates had somehow gotten it their heads that I was stalking the girl. I found out from the boy who was now in the habit of offering me gum. When I scowled at the sheer stupidity of the idea, he seemed amused and, yes, offered me gum. I politely declined.

I tried imagining the sequence of events that had led to the rumor. Almost certainly, several classmates had seen us together on different occasions, and they'd concluded I was always hanging around where she was. My peers, who generally considered me unpleasant, decided I was a malicious stalker. That was the best my imagination could do, but I thought I was close to what had happened.

However the rumor had started, it was ridiculous and entirely ungrounded in reality. And they all believed it. Disgusting. Almost everyone in class was looking at me and whispering about how I was a stalker and they needed to watch out.

I'll say it again: They disgusted me completely. Why did they believe their mob mentality was right by default? I'd bet that if thirty of them got together, they could murder someone and not even care. People who believed they were on the right side were capable of any deed. They didn't even realize they were acting like cogs in a machine and not individual people with humanity.

I wondered if they would escalate to bullying me, but that was me being overly self-conscious. Ultimately, our classmates' attentions were on her. Me hanging off her didn't change that. And I wasn't hanging off her, anyway.

They had no need to bother themselves with taking any action against me, and they had nothing to gain from doing so either. The only one who had any real interest in me was the best friend, who glared at me every day as she came into class. Being marked as her enemy was scary.

On Tuesday, I paid my second visit to the girl in the hospital, and when I reported the rumors to her, she clutched her hands to her pancreas and burst into laughter.

She said, "Oh, [Boy I'm Getting along With]-kun, you're all so hilarious."

"You think spreading malicious rumors behind peoples' backs is amusing? I didn't know you were so cruel."

"What's amusing is that nobody has any idea what to do with you. Do you even know why you're in that mess right now?"

I offered, "Because I'm spending time with you?"

"Trying to blame me, eh?" she said. She was sitting on her bed peeling a mandarin orange. "Wrong. They distrust you because you don't talk to them. They don't know what kind of person you are, [Boy I'm Getting along With]-kun. That's why they make those assumptions about you. If you want to put a stop to this, I think you're just going to have to make friends with them."

Neither I nor my classmates needed that. Once she was gone, I'd be alone again, and they would forget about me.

She said, "I think if they got to know who you were, they'd understand how fun you are. Besides, I don't believe they really think you're a bad person."

As I peeled my orange, I thought, *That's a dumb thing to say.*

I said, "Except for you and Kyōko-san, they all think of me as [Unremarkable Classmate]—at best."

She tilted her head, as if to drive home her point into the core of who I was. "Have you ever asked them?"

"I haven't. But I still think they do."

"You can't know if you don't ever ask. Until then, it's only in your head. You might not be right."

"I don't care if I'm right or not. I don't have anything to do with them, and it's *my* head, anyway. It's just what I think. I like to speculate what people think of me when they say my name."

"How self-absorbed is that? Is that what you are—one of those self-absorbed guys?"

"No, I'm the self-absorbed *prince,* and I hail from the land of the self-absorbed. You ought to show me respect."

Giving me a disinterested look, she hungrily ate her mandarin. I didn't expect she would understand my point of view; she was my opposite, after all.

Human interaction was her life; her expressions and her nature told me as much. In contrast, aside from my family, all my interactions with other people began and ended in my head. I imagined if they liked or disliked me, but I didn't particularly care which was true, as long as it didn't lead me into harm. I had given up on social interactions from day one. I was her complete opposite; nobody needed me around. Although if someone were to ask me if I was fine with that, I might have had trouble answering.

Having finished her mandarin, she neatly folded the peel into a ball and tossed it into the waste bin. The peel made it in, and she clenched her hand into a triumphant fist.

She said, "So then, what do you think I think of you?"

"A boy you're getting along with, I guess. Am I wrong?"

That was my honest answer, but she pursed her lips and said, "Wrong." Then, more to herself, she added, "Although that used to be what I thought of you."

I tilted my head quizzically. That was interesting phrasing. Did that mean instead of changing how she thought of me, she'd realized her feelings toward me were of a different nature than she'd first thought? My curiosity was piqued, if only by a little.

"All right," I said. "Then how do you think of me?"

"If I told you, there'd be no fun in it. Friendship and romances are fun *because* you don't know what you are to the other person."

"So I was right—you *do* think that way."

"Huh? Did we talk about this before?"

Maybe she really had forgotten. She brought her eyebrows together and made a puzzled, humorous expression. I laughed. A detached part of me observed myself being brought to genuine laughter by someone else. Partly suspicious, and partly impressed, I wondered when I had become that kind of person. I knew beyond any doubt the person who had caused that change was sitting in front of me. I doubted anyone could judge if the change was good or bad, but one thing was true: I had changed considerably.

Watching as I laughed, she narrowed her eyes and gently said, "I wish I could show everyone what an amazing person you are, [???]-kun."

That was quite a thing to say to the boy who had pinned her down, even if I would regret doing so for the rest of my life.

I said, "Everyone else can wait—just show Kyōko-san for now. She scares me."

"I've been trying to tell her. She's just being a good friend and worrying for me, you know. She thinks you're deceiving me."

"There must be something wrong with your powers of communication. I mean, she seems smart enough to understand, anyway."

"Whoa, such high praise." She gasped. "Don't tell me—you're looking to make her your plaything after I'm dead? Tacky."

I responded to her exaggerated reaction by giving her a disinterested look as I hungrily ate my mandarin. She shifted in bed as if that bored her, and I laughed again.

Then she said, "Time for today's magic trick."

This time, she'd practiced an illusion that involved manipulating a coin so it would disappear and reappear in her hands. The routine had a few hiccups, but just like last time, I thought she did an impressive job for a beginner—enough so that someone who didn't know anything about magic, like me, might wonder if she possessed a special talent for it.

She explained, "Well, all I do is practice! I don't have much time."

She'd left an opening for me to say something like, "You practice because all you have is time." I almost did, but I decided I wanted her to know I wasn't going to take such an easy opening, and instead I played it straight.

"In another year, you might be able to pull off some amazing tricks."

Mixed with odd pauses, she said, "Yeah, well... Sure!"

Maybe she didn't care for how I ignored her gag's setup. I stuck with it and honestly praised her effort and its results again. She smiled at me, in a good mood.

And just like that, my second visit to her in the hospital ended without any issue.

My journey home didn't go so smoothly.

If you asked me, no better place existed on this earth than the inside of a bookstore. On my trip home, as on many such occasions, I stopped in a bookstore to enjoy the cold air conditioning and search for a good book. Luckily, I hadn't come with a girl who would be waiting for me, so I was free to take as long as I pleased.

I had little to boast about myself, except for one ability in which I had total confidence: my concentration when I was reading a book. I could keep on reading forever, immune to my surroundings with only a few exceptions, like someone offering me a stick of gum or the school bell, which had become so familiar I could recognize its ring on a subconscious level. If I was an herbivore, I'd have been so engrossed by my fictional worlds that I wouldn't have noticed nearby predators, and I would surely be eaten quickly.

And so, until I finished the short story I was reading, and re-emerged into the real world where a disease was taking away the girl's life, I failed to notice the lion standing next to me.

I was so startled I nearly jumped. Wearing a large gym bag slung over her shoulder, the best friend was looking at an open paperback book in her hands. I knew, instinctively, that the entirety of her focus was on me, her prey.

I wondered if I could move quietly enough to escape. But that faint hope was quickly crushed.

"What is Sakura to you?"

She fired the question at me without even a word of greeting. Her words carried an edge sharp enough to bite through me if I answered wrong.

Cold sweat running down my back, I tried to figure out how I was supposed to answer. That was when I realized nothing prompted this interrogation except genuine concern for her friend. It was an honest question that left me no choice but to give an honest answer.

"I don't know."

The several seconds of silence that followed might have been her trying to decide how to respond, or she might have been working up the nerve to kill me on the spot. But the next thing I knew, her lion's claws were on my arm, and she yanked me toward her.

As I staggered forward, she said with a menacing voice, "No matter how she might seem, she's twice as easily hurt as other people. Stop getting close to her if you don't mean it. If you hurt her, I'll kill you."

I'll kill you. This wasn't the common, cheap threat employed by kids in grade school and junior high. This was the best friend's way of declaring that she was serious. I trembled.

The friend left without another word. My heart was racing, as hard as I tried to settle back down. I stood there, unable to move, until another classmate happened to wander into the bookstore and offer me gum.

That night, I tried to think seriously about what the girl meant to me.

But the answer still completely eluded me.

The day following my stint as prey at the bookstore, the girl sent me a text telling me to come visit her right away. This was unusual; for my past two visitations, she'd at least given me a day's notice. I thought something might have happened to her, but that proved not to be the case. When I arrived she gave me an unclouded smile and said, "How about you break me out of this hospital?"

What I read as urgency in her texts turned out to be excited impatience. She couldn't wait to let me in on her latest idea for mischief.

"No way," I said. "I don't want to be made into a murderer."

"It's okay. When the guy in a love story spirits his dying sweetheart from the hospital, everyone knows she's going to die on the trip. People will understand."

"By that logic, someone could be straddling a tub of scalding hot water saying he sure hopes nobody comes along and pushes him in, and I could push him in and still get away with it."

"Wouldn't you get away with it?"

"I wouldn't," I said. "I'd be arrested for criminal injury, or worse. So if you want to escape from the hospital, find some sweetheart who doesn't care if he shortens your life."

She clicked her teeth and spun a hair tie on her finger as if she was actually disappointed. That surprised me. Did she really think I would go along with something that put her in real danger? Even as a joke, I wouldn't have expected her to suggest such a foolish and life-threatening action.

Was she not joking? I looked at her face with that same familiar smile, and I felt uneasy. But the feeling quickly melted away.

She then suggested I help her escape from her room, and we went to a little store on the third floor. She walked in front of me as she towed along the rolling stand and IV bag so the tube wouldn't pull out from her arm. Seeing her like that, she truly looked like a sick person.

We were eating ice cream bars on a couch near the shop when she said, "Hey, do you know why sakura bloom in the spring?"

I wondered what had made her choose this subject.

I said, "You bloom in the spring? I don't even know what that means."

"Have I ever referred to myself in the third person? Did you confuse me with another girl named Sakura you've been hanging out with? I didn't know you were a cheat. Maybe you should die, too."

"Could you stop trying to drag me along just because you think heaven will be too dull without me? Now there's a thought—you should make sure your funeral is held on a tomobiki day."

Tomobiki days were superstitiously believed to be conducive to spreading one's fortune, whether good or ill, to one's friends.

"No way!" she said. "I want my friends to keep living."

"Maybe for your summer homework, you could write me a report on why you'd be fine with *me* dying. Anyway, you were asking why sakura trees bloomed in the spring. Isn't that just the kind of flower it is?"

I thought that to be a respectable guess, but she snorted derisively. I held back the strong urge to smoosh my lemon-flavored ice cream bar all over her nose.

Sensing my displeasure, she chuckled and got to her point.

"I'll tell you why. Did you know that after the sakura petals fall, the next buds grow within the next three months? But the buds sleep. They wait for warm weather to come, then they all bloom at once. In other words, sakura trees wait for the time they're supposed to bloom. Isn't that wonderful?"

I thought she was attributing too much conscious thought between the flowers' behavior. They were simply waiting for the insects and birds to come bearing pollen, but I didn't say anything. Instead, my thoughts went in a different direction.

I said, "Your name is a perfect fit."

"Because I'm a beautiful flower? You'll make me blush."

"No, because you're named after a flower that chooses to bloom in spring, just like you believe that our choices, not random chance, determine the people we encounter and the events in our lives."

She looked stunned for a moment, then became very happy and said, "Thank you."

I didn't understand why that made her so happy. I hadn't meant what I said as a compliment, just as an interesting fact, like how the clothes suited her when we were shopping.

She said, "Your name matches you well, too, [???]-kun."

"I don't know. Does it?"

"Look," she said, laughing proudly as she pointed back and forth at herself and me. "Death is next to you. Get it?" She was referring to the characters of my name. "Death and the spring tree?"

Once again, the feeling struck me that something was off with her; that sense had permeated our entire conversation.

She was nibbling at her watermelon popsicle, and as always, she seemed as if she was going to live forever. That hadn't changed, but there was something in her joke that reminded me of... I needed a moment to finish the thought, but then it came to me: She reminded me of a kid on the last day of summer vacation scrambling to finish a procrastinated independent study assignment.

Has something happened to her? I wondered with genuine concern. But I didn't ask. That hint of urgency I saw in her seemed only natural. She only had a year left to live. The times she managed to remain unperturbed were the oddity.

And so, I filed away the sense of wrongness I felt that day as something insignificant, a creation of my subjective point of view.

I thought I was right.

—— ✳ ——

But when she next asked me to visit on Saturday morning, that vague sense of wrongness manifested in visible form.

I arrived on time, and she noticed me right away and smiled and called my name. But her smile seemed slightly stiff.

Her expressive face was like a canvas on which her feelings were painted for me to see, and what I saw was nervousness. I sensed something bad was coming, and I didn't chase that premonition away.

My legs threatened to take a step back, but I steadied them and sat in my usual folding chair, when she took a deep breath and said something that didn't help shake my worry.

"Hey...[???]-kun?"

I hesitated, not sure where this was going. "Yeah, are you okay?"

"We only have to do one round," she said, reaching for a deck of cards on her bedside shelf. "But will you play truth or dare with me again?"

The devil's game.

"Why?" I asked. I sensed I could get away with refusing then and there, but I wanted to know why she suddenly proposed another round, and why she seemed so unnaturally fearful.

When she didn't answer me right away, I filled in for her, "There's either something you really want to ask me, or something you really want me to do, and it's something I would refuse if you asked me normally."

"That's...not it," she mumbled stiffly. "I think you might actually tell me if I asked you, but I can't quite bring myself to ask, so I thought I'd let luck decide."

What was making her act so out of character? I couldn't think of any dark secret I kept that would trouble her like this.

She stared into my eyes, as if to show me the depth of her determination. Strangely enough, my resistance evaporated under her gaze; maybe because I was the boat of reeds, or maybe something in her had affected me.

I made my decision.

"Well, I owe you for letting me borrow your book. I can play one round."

She said, "Thanks," as if she already knew I would accept, and she began shuffling the cards. Something was definitely off with her. Normally, she occupied every silence with chatter, but today she said only what she needed to. Curiosity and worry swirled in me like someone stirring fruit yogurt.

The rules were the same as last time, but because we were only playing a single round, we each picked five cards at random and placed them in a face down pile on her bed. We were to each choose one card.

After some serious struggle over choosing her card, she elected to go with one a little below the middle. I took the topmost card. Since this was a blind draw, each card was an equally valid choice. We also weren't taking the choice as seriously. She probably would have been mad to hear me say this, but I didn't care if I won or lost the game. If the match were decided by which of us was more determined to win—if that was the way the gods had created our reality to work—then she certainly would have won.

I imagined she would say life was fun because it didn't always work out that way.

We flipped our cards simultaneously, and she grimaced.

"Ah," she groaned, "I lost."

She clutched her blanket in her fists and seemed to be waiting for her crushing disappointment to pass. All I could do was watch. Eventually, she noticed my gaze, flung aside her disappointment, and smiled at me.

"Can't go back now! That's the way it goes!" she said. "That's what makes it fun."

"Oh, I have to think of a question now, don't I?"

"Go for it. I'll answer anything. Do you want to hear about my first kiss?"

"I'm not going to waste this chance on something less absorbing than an old sponge."

"But sponges do basically absorb things, don't they?"

"Sure. So? Did you think everything I say has to make sense?"

She laughed; she seemed to be in a good mood and normal enough. Maybe I'd just been overthinking things. Maybe some big secret hadn't been causing her to act strange. Her expression could change because of the slightest reasons, like alcohol or the weather. At least I hoped I'd been wrong.

Since I'd won the right to ask her a question—even if I hadn't particularly wanted it—I thought about what I should ask her. Her hobbies wouldn't have changed since the last time we played. I could ask another question to find out what had made her into the person she was. To be honest, one or two other questions had me more curious—like what she thought of me.

But I didn't have the courage to ask her those. Being with her had taught me that cowardice made me the person I was. In her bravery, I saw my opposite.

I looked at her as I searched for what to ask. She watched me back as she waited. Sitting quietly on her hospital bed, she seemed a little more like she was dying than before.

I decided on a question to shake away that premonition, and I asked it immediately.

"What does living mean to you?"

"Whoa," she said jokingly. "So serious."

But she looked thoughtful as she gazed upward and whispered to herself, "What does living mean to me?"

Just the sense that she was looking toward life—and not death—relieved my unease the slightest bit. I realized some part of me hadn't accepted she was going to die. I was a coward.

I thought back to how shaken I'd been when I saw the contents of her backpack in the hotel room, and the question she'd cornered me with at the end of that night.

"Oh!" she exclaimed, pointing a finger upward. "That's it. I've got it."

I listened close; I didn't want to miss her answer.

She said, "Living is..."

I waited.

"Sharing connections with other people. I think that's what we call living."

I felt suddenly aware of life.

Oh, I understand now.

The hairs rose on the back of my neck.

"To know someone, to get to like someone, to get to dislike someone, to enjoy being with someone, to hate being with someone, to hold hands with someone, to hug someone, to pass someone by. That's what it means to live. When you're all on your own, you don't know who you are. The people I like and dislike are who I am. The people I enjoy being with and the people I hate being with are who I am. Those connections are mine. They define my life as uniquely mine. I know I have feelings because of everyone around me. I know I have a body because other people can touch me. Those connections give me shape. I am alive here. I am alive now. That's what it means for someone to live—just as you and I have chosen to be alive here and now."

She had given her existence form through words, her gaze and her voice, her impassioned determination; vibrations of life that shook my soul.

"Well then," she said, "I got a little carried away there. What am I, an honoree giving a speech at an awards show?"

"No," I said flatly. "You're a patient in a hospital."

She puffed out her cheeks at me. This wasn't the right timing for a joke like that, but I hoped she'd forgive me.

I stayed quiet for a moment, then she said, "[???]-kun?"

Listening to her speech, I had discovered a genuine feeling building up inside my deepest depths. Once I recognized the feeling, I could see it had been right under my nose and nearly all encompassing, and yet—due to my cowardice—I had failed to notice it before.

And there it was, the answer I had been seeking for the past several days—no, that I had been seeking the whole time.

You...

I tried to suppress the thought as hard as I could.

"You really..."

"Oh, he speaks. Go on, [???]-kun."

"You really teach me so many different things."

"Whoa," she said. "Where'd that come from? You're making me blush."

"I mean it," I said. "Thank you."

"Are you sure you don't have a fever?"

She placed her palm on my forehead. My temperature was, of course, normal, and she tilted her head in confusion. Was she joking, or did she really think I might have had a fever? The thought was so silly, I laughed. She looked at me laughing, then put her palm to my head again. I laughed again. We repeated this for a while.

I was having so much fun because I was with her.

Once she finally accepted I didn't have a fever, I suggested that we share some sliced pineapple I'd brought for her by special request. She was delighted to see that I had.

We were eating the delicious pineapple when she sighed and said, "I've got no luck."

"Because of the truth or dare thing? Okay, how about this—if you ask me a question I can answer, I'll answer it for you. Forget the game."

"No, that was the result."

She left no room for arguing the matter. I still didn't have the slightest clue what she wanted to ask me.

After we finished our snack and I got her caught up with our summer school lessons, she showed off another magic trick. Not much time had passed since her last performance, so the illusion was a simple one involving props from a magic kit. Still, I was no expert, and I was impressed all the same. Feeling keenly aware of my previously unknown feelings, my eyes never left her through-out my class or her performance.

Afterward I said, "It's time for me to go. I need to get some lunch, anyway."

Wiggling her shoulders like a little kid, she protested, "What? You're leaving already?"

Maybe she hated being alone and bored in her hospital room even more than I'd thought.

I said, "Your lunch will be coming soon, won't it? And I wouldn't want Kyōko-san to show up and have me for hers."

"You think she'd eat your pancreas?"

"Possibly."

Imagining myself as a carnivore's dinner, I stood, and she shouted after me, "Wait!"

"Wait," she repeated. "Just do me one more favor."

She beckoned me closer. I approached without the slightest

bit of wariness, and without showing any maliciousness, hesitation, hidden motive, scheming, remorse, or responsibility, she half rose in her bed, leaned forward, and stretched her arms around me.

Her embrace came with so little warning that I didn't have time to be surprised. Instead, I stayed calmer than I would have believed possible. I rested my chin on her shoulder. She smelled sweet.

"So..." I said.

"This isn't like last time. I'm not playing a prank."

Another moment passed. "Then what is it?"

"You know, lately, I've just got this strange thing for wanting to feel other people's warmth."

Something in how she said that seemed to confirm my suspicions. I said, "Listen, there's something that's been bothering me."

"My bra size? 'Cause you can feel me against you, huh?"

"Dummy."

She laughed.

I said, "You've been acting strange. What's going on?"

Holding our embrace—well, with her embracing me at least—I awaited her answer. This time, I didn't feel like she was making a fool of me. I thought that if she wanted to use my body warmth, she could have it all she wanted.

Slowly, she shook her head two times.

"Nothing," she said. "Nothing at all."

Of course I didn't believe her. But I didn't have the courage to make her say anything she didn't want to.

She said, "I just want to enjoy the reality and normalcy you give to me."

"Oh," I said. Even if I had possessed some sort of misguided courage, whatever she was thinking wasn't mine to know in this moment.

She remained quiet, and after a time, I heard a wild beast growling behind my back.

Just when I thought our timing could never get worse.

"Sakura, how are—" the beast said. The growl became a roar. "It's *you!* Again?"

I freed myself from the girl's embrace and looked to the door, where her best friend was glaring at me with the face of a devil. I suspected I was making quite the face myself. As the friend advanced, I tried to take a step back, but the bed blocked my escape.

The friend was reaching to grab me by my collar, and I thought all hope was lost when I was rescued at the last moment. The girl quickly slid off her bed and hugged her friend tightly.

"Kyōko, calm down!" she said.

I said, "Okay, well, see you later," and made my escape out through her hospital room door. Was I going to have to run away every time I visited? As I scurried down the hall, I heard the friend shouting my name, but I smoothly ignored it, and thus ended my third visit. I wasn't sure, but I thought the girl's sweet scent lingered on my body.

On Sunday, the following night, I learned something that might have been what she was hiding from me. I'd say I saw this was coming, but I hadn't ever settled on any one theory in particular.

She told me by text.

Her hospitalization had been extended by two weeks.

Seven

S HE REACTED TO HER EXTENDED hospitalization with surprising indifference. The news had worried me, but seeing how she appeared to have expected the possibility reassured me a little. I wouldn't have admitted it to anyone, but I'd been alarmed.

I went to see her after classes on Tuesday afternoon. Summer school was almost over. "By the time I get out of here, summer vacation will be more than half over," she said, as if that was all that bothered her—or she wanted me to think that was all that bothered her.

It was a sunny day. Her hospital room, nice and cool, provided us shelter from the hot summer's daylight. Somehow, that shelter helped settle my nerves, even if the heat wasn't what was on my mind.

She asked, "How are things with Kyōko?"

"Okay, I guess. She's been glaring at me with a little more of a glint in her eye since last week. But whatever you said to her calmed her down, and she hasn't pounced on me again."

"Could you stop talking about my best friend like she's a wild beast?"

"Easy for you to say. I bet she's never looked at you like she does me. She's a wolf in sheep's clothing. Or more like a lion."

I hadn't told her about our run-in at the bookstore the week before.

I brought her some canned peaches for this visit. I poured the can's contents into a bowl, and we pecked away at the fruit. The sweet syrup reminded me of being a little kid.

The girl gazed out the window as she nibbled at the unnaturally yellow fruit.

"Why are you in a hospital on a beautiful day like this?" she asked. "You should go out and play dodgeball or something."

"First, you told me to come. Second, I haven't played dodgeball since I was in grade school. Third, I wouldn't have anyone to play it with. There's three reasons—you can take your pick."

"I'll take them all."

"Greedy, are you? I'll let you have the last peach then."

She gave me a childish grin, stabbed the last peach slice with her fork, and ate it in one bite. I carried the bowl, forks, and can to a sink in the corner of her room. Apparently, a nurse would come and clean up for us. Between not having to do our own dishes and the room service meals, if it weren't for her sickness, this might have felt like a VIP suite.

As part of her VIP package, I taught her our class materials at no charge, and although she seemed to want to be doing anything else, she took her notes diligently. When I asked her why she needed to study—she wouldn't be taking any college entrance exams, after all—she explained that if her grades suddenly plummeted, everyone around her would think that something was up. I realized why I never particularly cared about studying.

There was no magic show today. That was understandable; I wouldn't have expected her to have another trick ready so soon. She told me she was practicing something special and that I should look forward to it.

"I'll be waiting with bated breath," I said.

"How *do* you bait your breath? Do you eat a worm or something?"

"Oh no, have you gotten too dumb to recognize common sayings? You have it bad enough already—now you've got a brain virus too."

"If you call someone else dumb, that makes you the dumb one," she said.

"It doesn't work like that. If I say you're sick, that doesn't make me the sick one."

"Sure it does. You should drop dead. Look, I'm going to die now. See? It works."

"I thought I told you to stop dragging me down with you."

I was glad to have our typical nonsense. Our little jokes felt like proof that everything was normal.

If I had more experience with other people, I might not have been so reassured by something so trivial.

I happened to glance at the corner of her room. The flooring had darkened at the edges along the wall, as if fragments of the previous patients' illnesses had accumulated there and wouldn't let go.

I slowly shifted my gaze from the corner back to the girl. She said my name, and my eyes landed on her a little faster.

"[???]-kun, do you have any plans for summer break?"

"Just coming here and reading books at home. And doing homework."

"That's all? C'mon, it's vacation. Do something. Since I won't be going on a trip with Kyōko, why don't you go with her instead?"

"I don't have a license to handle dangerous animals. How come you're not going on a trip with her?"

"Now that I'm in here longer, the timing doesn't work. The second half of break she'll be busy with volleyball." She smiled sadly. "I really wanted to go on another trip."

My breath caught. The whole room seemed to darken, air and all, and some unwanted presence stirred in my chest. I nearly coughed. I was only able to hold it down by taking a quick drink of my bottled tea.

What did she say?

I replayed what she said in my mind, like I was some detective in a novel and she was the prime suspect.

I must have looked troubled. Her smile vanished, and she tilted her head at me quizzically.

But I was the one with the question, which tumbled out: "Why did you phrase that like you're never going to be able to go on a trip again?"

She looked caught off guard, wide-eyed, like a pigeon shot by a peashooter.

Finally, she said, "Did I?"

"You did."

"Oh. Well, I guess sometimes even I worry, that's all."

"Hey..." I said. I wondered what kind of face I was making. The waves of dread I'd hidden since my last visit now threatened to leap from my lips. I tried to cover my mouth with my hand to keep from talking, but my hand didn't get there in time.

I said, "You're not going to die, right?"

"Huh? Sure I am. I'm going to die, and so will you."

"That's not what I mean."

"If you're talking about my pancreas, then yes, I am going to die from my disease."

"That's not what I mean!"

I pounded my fists on the edge of her bed and stood. I didn't mean to—it just happened. My folding chair slid back, metal legs scraping on the floor with an awful screech. My eyes were locked on hers. She looked truly shocked. So was I. What was happening to me?

My throat had gone dry and scratchy, but I managed to squeeze out one more sentence, like the last drop from a bottle.

"You're not going to die *yet*, right?"

Still in shock, she didn't respond. The room filled with silence, a scary presence that compelled me to keep talking.

"You've been acting strange."

Still no response.

"You're hiding something from me," I said. The words began tumbling out faster than I had ever spoken before. "But I see through it. The truth or dare game, you suddenly hugging me. When I asked you if something was going on, your response was weird, too. Did you think I wouldn't notice how long you took to answer? You're sick. You're in a hospital. I worry about you, you know?"

When I finally finished, I was short of breath, and not just because I hadn't paused to take any breaths. I was flustered; I didn't know what to do anymore—about her, or about me intruding on her.

She was still dumbstruck, staring at me. Seeing that I wasn't the most confused person in the room, I managed to get a small hold of myself, and I sat back in my chair and slackened my grip on her bedsheets.

I watched her face. Her eyes were wide open, and her lips were tight. I wondered if she would try to change the subject again. If she did, what would I do? Did I possess the courage to press her any further? If I did, would it even matter?

What did I even *want* to do?

I was lost in my thoughts when she gave me the answer.

Her expression always changed so rapidly. I didn't know what look would replace her current one of blank surprise, but I expected that, when it happened, the change would come suddenly.

I was wrong. This time, her expression changed its color slowly. The corners of her closed lips lifted at a snail's pace. Her wide eyes narrowed with the speed of a curtain lowering at the end of a play. Her stiffened cheeks rose as fast as ice melted.

She gave me a smile that would have taken me more than a lifetime to replicate.

"Shall I tell you?" she asked. "What's going on?"

"Yes," I said with the trepidation of a kid who was about to incur an adult's wrath.

Her lips parted, and she sounded content as she answered, "Nothing at all. I've just been thinking about you."

"About me?"

"Yes. I wasn't even going to ask you anything special in that truth or dare game. If I was forced to say what's been on my mind, it's that I want us to get even closer."

"Really?" I asked with a skeptical tone.

"Really. I don't lie to you."

She may have just been telling me what I wanted to hear, but I couldn't entirely hide my relief. The tension melted from my shoulders. I knew I was being naïve, but I believed her.

She laughed, low and slow.

"What?" I asked.

"I was just thinking about how happy I am. I could just die now."

"You better not."

"Do you want me to keep living?"

I said, "Yes."

Keeping her eyes on me, she giggled. She sounded exceedingly happy, even for her. "I never imagined you would need me that much. I don't think anything could ever make me happier. Why, with a shut-in like you, I'm probably the first person you've ever needed."

"Who are you calling a shut-in?" I said, going along with her joke, but I felt so mortified I thought my face might explode. I was embarrassed for worrying about her, for not wanting to lose her, for needing her. All of that was true, but putting those emotions into words embarrassed me vastly more than when they were just feelings. I felt like all the blood in my body was racing to the top of my head. Maybe I would die first after all. Somehow, I managed to take deep breaths to expel the heat of my embarrassment.

Apparently, she didn't feel like giving me time to recompose myself. Still radiating happiness, she continued, "You thought I was acting strange because I was about to die? And I was keeping it from you?"

"Yeah. Your hospitalization was suddenly extended, too."

She rolled on her bed, laughing so hard I thought her IV might pop out of her arm. I could only be laughed at so long before I started getting annoyed.

"It's your fault," I protested. "You're the one who made me think that."

"I told you I still had time, didn't I? If I was going to die so soon, why would I keep practicing magic? That explains why you were reading so much into my pauses and everything. You've been reading too many novels."

When she'd finished talking, she laughed again and said, "Don't worry, I'll tell you when I'm going to die."

Still more laughter. She'd laughed at me so long I started feeling silly, too. I was forced to admit how tremendous my mistake had been.

She said, "When I die, you'd better eat my pancreas."

"What if I just ate the bad parts? Would you keep living then? Maybe I should go ahead and eat your pancreas for you now."

"You want me to keep living?"

"Very much."

I was glad my humor was dry enough that I could speak the truth and have it come across as a joke. If she took the truth as truth, I may have been too ashamed to ever come out in public again.

I didn't really know how she took it, but she jokingly squealed with delight and spread open her arms to me. "Maybe you've taken an interest in other people's warmth, too," she said, snickering.

I could tell she was joking because of her laugh. I joked in my own way, by obliging.

I stood and approached her, and—as a joke—I put my arms around her for the first time. She pretended to be embarrassed and put her arms around me. I'll ask you not to be so ungraceful as to wonder what this all meant. If you think about the logic behind a joke too hard, you'll only spoil it.

We held each other like that for a while, when I wondered, "Strange. Kyōko-san's timing must be off today. She isn't showing up."

"She has volleyball today. What do you see her as, anyway?"

"A demon who comes to tear us apart."

We laughed, and the timing felt right to let her go. I did, but before she released her embrace, she gave me one more tight squeeze. We saw each other's faces, beet red from our joke, and laughed again.

Once we'd settled down, she abruptly said, "Speaking of me dying..."

"You know, that might be the first time anyone started a conversation with those words."

"I've been thinking about starting to write my goodbyes for everyone to read when I'm gone."

"Aren't you getting ahead of yourself?" I asked. "Or maybe you *were* lying when you said you still had time."

"No," she said, "I just want to do it right. That means revising and rewriting, so I want to start the rough drafts now."

"That sounds like a good idea. I've heard revising a novel can take longer than writing the first draft."

"See, I knew I had it right. I hope you'll like what I write for you."

I said, "I can't wait."

"You mean you want me to die faster? That's mean. Of course, I know you don't actually want me to die, because you need me too badly."

She gave me a grin. I considered nodding in agreement, but I'd had about all the sentimentality I could handle for one day. I gave her a bored look instead, but she persisted in grinning at me. Maybe that was a symptom of her illness.

She said, "Tell you what. Since I caused you to worry needlessly, I'll make it up to you by visiting you first thing after I'm released."

"If that's an apology, it doesn't sound very humble."

"So you don't want to see me?"

"I don't not want to see you."

"[???]-kun, that's just like you."

What was like me? I felt like I had a vague impression of what she meant by that, so I didn't ask.

She said, "The day I get discharged, I have to go home first, but after that, in the afternoon, I'll be free."

"What do you want to do?"

"I don't know yet. You'll come back a few times before then, won't you? We can think about it."

That worked for me.

Over the next two weeks, we settled on a plan for our "date," as she called it, even if it wasn't. She wanted to go to the ocean. We would also stop at a café, location to be determined, where she could show me her greatest magic trick.

By setting plans for what we would do after she got out of the hospital, I felt as if we were tempting fate for something worse to happen—a sudden decline of her condition, for example. But nothing eventful occurred, and the days simply passed by until she was able to go home. Maybe she was right; maybe I had read too many novels.

During those two weeks, I went to see her four more times. One time, I ran into her friend. Twice, she laughed so hard her bed shook. Three times, she whined when the time came for me to leave. Four times, I put my arms around her. Not once did it become routine.

We joked a lot, laughed a lot, insulted each other a lot, and admired each other a lot. I grew fond of our uneventful days together. They reminded me of being a little kid again.

A detached part of me observed this change with surprise.

This is what I would have explained to that observer: I was enjoying human contact. For the first time in my life, I was spending time with someone without ever thinking I'd rather be alone.

Surely no one else in the world had ever been so deeply moved by human contact as I was during those two weeks. For me, the four days we were together in her hospital room comprised the entirety of those two weeks. Everything else just fell away.

And four days wasn't a long wait at all.

The day she was scheduled to be released from the hospital, I woke up early. Most days, I woke up early in the morning, rain or shine, whether I had plans or not. Today, the sun shone, and I had plans. I opened my bedroom window and let the fresh air into my room. I gazed off, as if I could see the flowing currents. The morning felt good.

Downstairs, I washed my face, and when I went to the living room, my father was on his way out. I thanked him for going to work, and he looked happy and slapped me on the back before he went out the door. He was always full of energy, year-round. I always wondered how someone like me could have been born to a father like him.

My breakfast was already waiting for me on the dining table. I said, "Itadakimasu" to my mother, giving appreciation for the meal, then I said it again to my food on the table before eating her miso soup. I really liked her soup.

As I enjoyed my breakfast, my mom finished up with the dishes and sat across the table, where she began drinking a cup of coffee.

"Hey, you," she said.

"What?"

"When did you get a girlfriend?"

"Huh?"

What had gotten into her? Was that seriously the first thing she wanted to say to me in the morning?

She said, "If it's not a girlfriend, then it must be someone you like. Whatever it is, you should bring her over."

"It's neither, and I won't."

"Hmmm. I would have sworn."

I wondered where she had gotten that idea. I guessed it was her parental intuition at work. Even if she was wrong.

She said, "Just a friend, then."

That wasn't right either.

"Well, it doesn't matter what she is," my mother said. "I'm just glad someone has come along who can see you for who you are."

"Um... Okay?"

"Did you think I hadn't seen through your lie? Don't underestimate your mother."

I stared at her. I appreciated my mother, but I had indeed completely underestimated her. Her eyes had a strength and a brightness that mine didn't, and she really did look happy for me. I felt put in my place. I smiled with just the corners of my lips. My mom had already turned her attention to the TV as she continued sipping her coffee.

Since I wasn't supposed to meet the girl until the afternoon, I spent all morning reading. The book she'd lent me, *The Little Prince*, was still waiting its turn. On my bed, I read a mystery novel I'd bought not that long ago.

The hours passed quickly, and a little before noon I changed into some simple street clothes and left the house. I wanted to go book shopping first, so I arrived at the train station quite a bit early and went into a large bookstore nearby.

I browsed the store for a while, bought one book, then went to the café where we were to meet. The place was a short walk from the station, but since this was a weekday, there were plenty of open tables. I ordered an iced coffee and claimed a seat by the window. I was about an hour early.

The coffee shop was pleasantly cool, but I felt hot on the inside, and the iced coffee was refreshing as it went down. The coolness spread through me, as if it was circulating through my body; of course, that was only in my imagination. If the coffee really did circulate throughout my body, I'd be the one who died first.

Between the A/C and iced coffee, I managed to stop sweating, and soon my stomach began growling. Thanks to my healthy lifestyle, my appetite was right on schedule for lunch. I thought about ordering something to eat, but I'd promised to have lunch with her. If I satisfied my hunger now, and she whisked me away to another all-you-can-eat place, I'd regret my decision. She could have that effect sometimes.

I thought back to when she dragged me out to lunch those two days in a row, and I chuckled. That was more than a month ago now.

Deciding to wait for her responsibly, I took out my current paperback and put the book on the table.

I'd intended to read the novel, but my gaze drifted outside; I didn't know why. If I had to give a reason, all I could say was I just felt like it, which was the sort of carefree reason I expected from her, not myself.

Outside, people passed by each other in the bright daylight. A man looked like he was overheating in his suit; why didn't he take off his jacket? A young woman in a tank top trotted toward the train station; was she off to do something fun? A high-school aged boy and girl walked together, holding hands; a couple. A mother pushed her baby along in a stroller and—

I noticed what I was doing, and I was taken aback.

The people outside were strangers. I would likely never have any connection to them the rest of my life.

If they were strangers, why was I thinking about them? I wouldn't have done that before.

I thought I had no interest in the people around me. Or rather, I had decided not to take any interest in them.

I chuckled to myself. Had I changed this much? I was enjoying this, and I laughed again.

I pictured the face of the girl I was waiting to join me.

She had changed me. She'd changed me, and I knew it.

The day we met—not when we got put in the same class in school, but when we actually met—I was put on a path of change, in who I was, in the course my life would take, and in my views on life and death.

Then I remembered what she would say if she heard those thoughts—that I had made the choice to change myself.

I chose to pick up the lost book.

I chose to open that book.

I chose to talk to her.

I chose to train her how to be a student librarian.

I chose to accept her invitation. I chose to eat with her.

I chose to walk next to her. I chose to go on a trip with her.

I chose to take that trip wherever she wanted to go. I chose to sleep in the same room as her.

I chose truth. I chose dare.

I chose to sleep in the same bed with her.

I chose to eat the breakfast she didn't finish. I chose to watch the street performer with her.

I chose to suggest she learn magic.

I chose to buy her the Ultraman figure. I chose the souvenir we ate on the train.

I chose to tell her I had fun on the trip.

I chose to go to her house.

I chose to play shogi. I chose to push her away from me.

I chose to pin her to the bed. I chose to hurt the class representative.

I chose to yield to him. I chose to make up with her.

I chose to visit her in the hospital. I chose the gifts to bring.

I chose to teach her what I had learned in class. I chose when to go home.

I chose to run from her best friend. I chose to watch her magic trick.

I chose to play truth or dare. I chose my question.

I chose not to run from her arms. I chose to get an explanation from her.

I chose to laugh with her. I chose to embrace her.

Again and again, at every point along the way, I made a choice.

I could have made different choices, and the ones I made were of my own free will and nothing else. My free will brought me here—as a changed person.

I came to a realization:

No one was a boat of reeds, not even me. We choose whether to flow with the currents or turn against them.

She had taught me that. Even though she would soon die, she looked more to the future than anyone else, and she took possession over her life. She loved the world, she loved its people, and she loved herself.

Again I had that thought.

You teach me so much that—

My phone vibrated in my pocket.

I just got home! I think I might be a little late. Sorry! 😅 I'll wear something cute for you! 💕

I thought for a moment, then replied half-jokingly.

Congrats on escaping the hospital. I was just thinking of you.

Her reply came right away.

Are you trying to say something to make me happy?
What's wrong, are you sick? 😌

I waited a little bit before responding.

Unlike you, I'm healthy.

Meanie! You hurt my feelings. Now you have to make it
up to me by saying something you like about me!

I can't think of anything, but I don't know if the problem is
with me or with you.

100% you. Stop stalling.

I placed my cell phone on the table, crossed my arms, and
thought. Something I liked about her... There were more than I
could count. More than could fit in my phone's memory.

I had truly learned so much from her. She taught me about
things I'd never known.

Like texting back and forth. She showed me how much fun
talking to another person could be, and how I could try to find
things to say that would get an entertaining response from her.

The parts of her that were incredible—the things that gave
her charm—had absolutely nothing to do with her shortened

life. I was sure she had always been this person. Maybe her viewpoint had taken a slightly firmer shape, and her words took on more richness, but I believed who she was at her core would have been just the same if she was to die the next year or keep on living.

She was amazing just how she was. That in and of itself was amazing.

I was amazed every time she taught me something new. She was my direct opposite. She could easily declare and do things I was too cowardly and withdrawn to do myself.

I took my phone in my hand.

You're truly an amazing person.

That's what I'd been thinking for a long time. But I hadn't been able to find the right words to neatly contain how I felt.

But then, when she taught me what living meant to her, I understood.

She completed my heart.

I...

I want to be you.

To be someone who could know other people, and who could be known.

To be someone who could love other people, and who could be loved.

I'd finally found words to fit how I felt, and they seemed to permeate my being. A smile came to my lips.

How did I become like you?

How can I become more like you?

A thought came to me—a vague recollection of a weird old saying that seemed to be made just for this purpose.

I searched my memory, found the phrase, and decided to send it to her.

I want to brew a potion from the dirt under your nails.

I determinedly typed those words but immediately deleted them. Something told me that an idiom wasn't interesting enough. I thought there must be something else, something more appropriate, that I could say to make her happy.

As I thought it over once more, the words came to me from a corner of my memory—or maybe the center of it.

I felt elation at finding those words, along with more than a little pride.

There was no better message to send her than this.

Nothing else so perfectly summed up my being.

I...

I want to eat your pancreas.

I sent the message to her phone, placed mine back on the table, and waited excitedly for her reply. If I'd told myself just a few months ago I would be sitting here, impatiently waiting for anyone's reply about anything, I wouldn't have believed it. Well, the me of a few months ago made the choices that brought me here, so he had no right to complain.

I waited.

And I waited.

But her reply didn't come.

Time passed, and my hunger grew.

When the clock ticked past the time we were to meet, I began looking forward to hearing her reply in person.

But like her reply, she didn't come either.

For thirty minutes, I didn't think anything of it.

After an hour or two, I grew restless with worry. How could I not?

After three hours, I tried calling her. She didn't answer.

After four hours, the sky was beginning to change color. I left the café; I knew something must have happened, but I didn't know what. I felt an ill-defined fear but had no way of dispelling it. I texted her again and went home.

At home, I told myself her parents had probably forced her to do something else today. That was the only way I could shake my fear.

I was restless and uneasy. Later, I'd wish I could have frozen time and stayed that way.

"Later" came too quickly. I was sitting at the table and watching TV, picking disinterestedly at my dinner, as worry had replaced my appetite.

That's when I learned why she hadn't come.

She had lied.

I had lied, too.

She broke her word by not telling me when she would die.

I broke my word by not returning the book I'd borrowed and the money I owed her.

I would never be with her again.

The news was on.

My classmate, Yamauchi Sakura, had been discovered, collapsed in an alleyway in a residential area by a local resident.

After being found, she had been rushed by ambulance to a hospital, but despite the best efforts to resuscitate her, she passed away.

The newscaster reported these facts without any emotion.

My unused chopsticks slipped from my fingers and dropped to the floor.

When they found her, she had been stabbed by a common kitchen knife.

She had become another victim of the random killer from the neighboring prefecture.

The police quickly apprehended the murderer. He was nobody at all.

—— ✳ ——

She was dead.

I had been naïve.

Even after everything, I had still been naïve.

I took it for granted that she had one year left.

She might have taken that for granted, too.

At the very least, I had failed to realize no one was guaranteed a tomorrow.

I assumed, as a matter of course, that a girl with little time left would at least have a tomorrow.

I assumed my death had not yet been assigned, and could come at any time, but if she had only been given a year to live, she was at least promised a tomorrow.

What kind of fool's logic was that?

I believed the world would at least spare the life of a girl who had little life left.

Of course, life doesn't work that way. It never has.

The world doesn't discriminate.

The world doesn't pull its punches from any of us; not people healthy like me, and not people with fatal diseases like her.

We had been wrong. We had been stupid.

But who could blame us?

Once a TV serial was announced to end, the show always aired until the finale.

Once a manga's final chapter was advertised, the manga always ran until the end.

Once the last movie in a series had a preview, that movie always came to the theaters.

Everyone just assumed these things to be true. Life had taught us those expectations.

I had assumed them, too.

I believed stories never ended before the last page.

She probably would have laughed at me and told me I read too much.

I wouldn't have minded her laughing at me.

I wanted—and had intended—to read this story to the end.

But her story was over; the final pages left blank.

Foreshadowing never to be paid off. Story threads left dangling. Plot twists never revealed.

I would never know how her story was to turn out.

What happened to her rope and the prank she'd planned?

What was her big magic trick?

What did she really think of me?

I would never find out.

At least, that's what I thought.

That was the reality I'd resigned myself to accept after she died.

But later, I realized that wasn't really true.

I hadn't gone to visit her house after her funeral and after her cremation.

I stayed in my room every day reading my books.

It took me ten days to find a reason to visit her house, and the courage to do so.

At the tail end of summer vacation, I remember something.

There might be a way for me to read the last pages of her story.

The key is in the object that brought us together in the first place.

I need to read *Living with Dying*.

Eight

I<small>T'S RAINING</small>, and the dreary weather is unlikely to inspire any summer homework procrastinators to change their ways, no matter how soon school will be starting again.

At least, that's my first impression as I wake up on the eleventh morning of her absence. I suppose I wouldn't really know—I'm the type who always finishes his summer homework straight away, and I've never been one to practice that last-minute scramble.

I go downstairs to wash my face. My father, about to leave for work, joins me at the sink and inspects his appearance in the mirror. We exchange a quick good morning, and he slaps me on the back. I don't know what the gesture is meant to communicate, and trying to figure out seems like more of a hassle than it's worth.

I greet my mother in the kitchen and sit at the dining table, where my usual breakfast is already waiting. I touch my hands together in a perfunctory prayer and eat my miso soup. My mom's soup is always tasty, no matter what else is happening in the world.

I continue eating my breakfast, and my mom comes over to the table with her fragrant cup of coffee in hand. I glance at her. She's looking at me.

She says, "You're going out today, aren't you?"

"Yeah. In the afternoon."

"Take this."

She casually hands me a white envelope. I take it and look inside. A single 10,000-yen note is inside. I look at my mother in surprise.

"Is this...?"

"Go and say your goodbyes, dear."

She returns her attention to the television, laughing at some TV personality's dumb joke. I finish my breakfast in silence and take the white envelope back to my room. My mom doesn't say anything else.

I pass the rest of the morning in my room before changing into my school uniform to go out. I've heard it's better if you go in school dress rather than street clothes. I guess the uniform helps the family know you're not just some stranger.

I return to the downstairs washroom to straighten out my bedhead. My mom has already left for work.

Back in my room, I put everything I need in my school bag: the white envelope, my cell phone, *The Little Prince*. I don't yet have the money to pay back what I borrowed from her—that will have to wait.

I step outside where the heavy rain is bouncing off the pavement, and in no time, several droplets perch on my pant legs. I go on foot, because I can't ride my bicycle and hold an umbrella at the same time.

Few people are out on the street at noon on a stormy weekday. I walk to the school in silence.

Near the school, I stop in a neighborhood convenience store to buy an envelope appropriate for a funeral offering. The store has a small table where customers can sit and eat, and I use it to transfer the money from the plain white envelope my mother gave me.

A short walk from the school, I enter a residential area, where I'm struck by a fairly tasteless thought.

Oh, she got killed somewhere around here.

I'm alone on the street. Maybe that's how it was that day, too, when she was stabbed. Not by somebody she'd angered, not by somebody seeking to spare her from her illness, but by somebody whose face or name she didn't know.

Oddly, I don't feel any sense of guilt over what happened. If I was to look for reasons to blame myself, I could find them—if I hadn't made plans with her that day, she wouldn't have died, for example—but I understand that won't change anything.

Maybe you think that sort of logical thinking makes me heartless, or unfeeling. Who, me?

I'm sad.

I'm hurt, but the pain won't break me. Of course losing her makes me sad, but there are people out there whose grief eclipses mine, like her family, whom I'm on my way to visit; her best friend; maybe even the class representative. When I think of them, I can't help but shut out some of my own sadness.

Besides, falling to pieces won't bring her back. The only reasonable action is to keep myself together.

I continue walking through the rain, and I pass the place where I got punched.

As I approach her house, I'm not particularly nervous. My only worry, and it's a minor one, is what I'll do if no one is home.

Standing before her front door for the second time in my life, I push the button on the intercom without hesitation. Before long, a response comes; someone's home. Good.

"Who is it?" says a woman's muffled voice.

I give her my family name and say I'm Sakura-san's classmate. The woman says, "Oh," and there's a pause. Then, "Just a moment," and the intercom clicks off.

I wait in the rain until the door opens, revealing a slender woman. She must be the girl's mother. Aside from the tiredness in her face, she looks like her daughter. I greet her, and with a stilted expression, she invites me inside. I fold up my umbrella and follow her in.

She shuts the front door, and I offer a proper bow.

"I'm sorry to come unannounced," I say. "I wasn't able to attend the wake or the funeral, but I was hoping I could at least offer some incense."

She seems to accept what I say, even if it's not entirely true. Her expression stiffens again, but she says, "It's fine. You're not interrupting anything—no one else is home right now. I'm sure Sakura will be happy to see you."

I think, *She'd have to be here to be happy,* but I would never say it.

I remove my shoes and step in from the entryway. Her house feels bigger and colder than when I came here before, but maybe that's just my imagination.

Her mother leads me into the living room; I didn't come into this room last time.

She says, "You probably want to pay your respects to her first."

I nod, and she guides me to a tatami-mat room next to the living room. When I see the memorial arrangement, I feel unsteady, inside and out, but I manage to keep walking, albeit with shaky, unnatural footsteps. I approach a wooden bookshelf on which various items have been placed.

Her mother kneels, retrieves a match from a bottom shelf, and lights a candle.

"Sakura," she says softly to a picture of the girl on the center shelf. "A friend has come to see you."

Her voice, hollow and thin, reaches nowhere but my ears.

She invites me to sit on a floor cushion and I do.

Like it or not, I'm faced with the girl's picture.

She's smiling. I can still hear her laugh.

I can't do this.

Looking away from her picture, I ring a small high-pitched bell that has some religious name I forget, and I put my hands together.

I feel like I should know what I want to pray for, but I can't think of anything.

I finish paying my respects to her and turn to her mother, who is sitting on the tatami mat next to me. I slide off my cushion and match her position. She gives me an exhausted but genuine smile.

I tell her, "I have something I borrowed from your daughter. Is it all right if I return it to you?"

"You have something of hers? Well, yes, you may. What is it?"

I reach into my bag to retrieve *The Little Prince* and hand it to her. She seems to recognize the book, and she holds it to her chest for a moment before placing the paperback next to the girl's picture, as if in offering.

Bowing her head respectfully, she says, "Thank you, truly, for being her friend."

I'm not sure how to respond. Eventually, I say, "Actually, Sakura-san was very good to me. She was always so cheerful and full of life. She brightened my mood whenever I was with her."

She hesitates before saying, "Yes... She was full of life."

Oh, that's right. No one outside her family is supposed to know about her pancreas.

I consider keeping my knowledge a secret, but I realize I'm going to have to come clean either way if I want to accomplish what I'm here to do.

I don't know how the truth will affect her family, and the part of me with a conscience considers stopping, but I quickly squash that sentiment and say, "There's something I have to tell you."

"Oh?"

Her face is kind and sad. I squash my conscience again.

"The truth is, I... I knew about her illness."

"What?"

Her expression is as surprised as I'd expected.

"She told me about it. I never imagined that...this would happen."

Still in stunned silence, she puts her hand over her mouth. It's true, then: The girl hadn't told her family she'd revealed her illness to anyone else. I suspected as much. When I visited her in the hospital, she allowed me to cross paths with her friend, but made sure I never ran into her family. That was one awkwardness she spared me.

I explain, "I happened to run into her at the hospital one day. That was when she told me. I don't know why she did."

Her mother stays quiet, letting me speak, and so I continue.

"She kept it a secret from all our other classmates. I know this must come as a great surprise, and I'm sorry for springing it on you."

It's time to get to the point.

"I came here for more than paying my respects. I have another favor to ask you. She kept a book—a sort of journal—after she got sick. I'm hoping you'll let me read it."

More silence.

"Living with Dying," I say, and it's like I flipped a switch.

Yamauchi Sakura's mother, still holding her hand to her mouth, begins to cry. Quietly, quietly, holding back any sound, she cries, tears flowing from both eyes.

I don't understand why that made her cry. I made her sad, I can see that much. But for reasons I don't comprehend, finding out I knew about the illness has triggered an even deeper sorrow than was already burdening her. Without understanding why, I can't find the right words to comfort her. Instead, I quietly wait.

She's still crying when she stares into my eyes and begins to explain.

"It's you," she says.

What does that mean?

"Thank you," she says. "Thank you... I'm so happy you've come."

I'm even more confused than before. Too unsure to speak, all I can do is watch her cry.

"Please, wait here," she says.

She stands and vanishes into some other part of the house. Alone now, I search for the meaning behind her tears and what she said. Try as I might, nothing comes to mind.

She returns before I find an answer. In her hand is a familiar paperback-sized book.

She says, "This is it, right?"

Still in tears, she gently places the book on the tatami floor and turns it toward me. It is indeed the book, the girl's constant companion. But for one exception, she had kept its contents secret from me the whole time.

"Yes, that's it," I say. "*Living with Dying*. She told me it was a journal she started when she found out she was sick. She never let me read it, but she told me she would make her writings public after she died. Did she ever say something like that to you?"

Her mother nods once, then again, and she keeps nodding. Each time, teardrops fall onto the tatami mats and her pale skirt.

I bow my head and plead, "Please. May I read it?"

"Yes. Yes, of course."

"Thank you."

"Sakura left it for you. Specifically you."

My hand is reaching for the book when I reflexively freeze, caught by surprise. I look to her mother's face.

"What?" I say.

Her crying intensifies, and she begins to speak between her sobs.

"Sakura told me. She said that when she...when she died, I was to give it to a certain person. She said he'd know about her sickness. He'd know the title of her book."

Her tears keep falling and evaporating into the air. All I can do is continue listening. Beside me, the girl's smiling photograph watches us.

"She said that he...that he'd probably be too afraid to come to her funeral. But he would come for the book. Until then, we weren't to show it to anyone outside our family. I still remember... exactly how she told me. It feels so long ago now."

She covers her face with both hands now and breaks down completely. I'm still dumbfounded. This isn't what the girl told me. She left the book...to me?

Memories of our time together flash through my mind.

Her mother's voice squeaks out through her tears.

"Thank you. Thank you. Because of you, she... With you, she..."

Unable to restrain myself any longer, I pick the book up off the floor. Nobody stops me.

— ✳ —

The first pages are a sort of monologue. She would have been in junior high.

November 29—

I don't want to write about really depressing stuff, so I'll get this part out of the way. When I found out I was sick, my mind went blank, and I didn't know how to handle it. I got scared and cried. I got mad and took it out on my family. I did a lot of different things. First, I want to apologize to my family. I'm sorry. And thank you for staying with me until I settled back down. [...]

December 4—

It's been cold lately. I've been doing a lot of thinking since I found out about my illness. For one thing, I've decided not to resent my fate. That's why I didn't name this book about fighting against my illness, but rather, living with it. [...]

After that, there's an entry every few days describing various events in her life. This goes on for a few years, and each entry is fairly short. I don't suspect anything in this part contains the answers I seek, and I decide to skim the entries for now. A few stand out to me, however.

October 12—

I got a new boyfriend. I'm not sure how I feel about it.

If we stay together for a while, will I have to tell him about my illness? I don't want to.

January 3—
We broke up. Not an auspicious start to the new year. Kyōko consoled me.

January 20—
Eventually, I'll have to tell Kyōko about my illness. But not until the very end. I want us to still have fun together. I'd better apologize here in case she ever reads this. Kyōko, I'm sorry I didn't tell you I was dying.

She writes about finishing ninth grade, moving on to high school, and celebrates this time of her life with Kyōko-san. A year passes, and she's a second-year student. She senses her end is coming, but she still strives to live a joyful life. Her words etch themselves deep in my soul.

June 15—
I'm more and more a high school student now. I thought hard about joining a club but eventually decided not to. Some of the cultural clubs sounded better than the sports clubs, but I finally went with the "going home after school club." I need to prioritize the time I can spend with my family and friends. Kyōko is back on the volleyball team again, playing hard every day. You go, Kyōko!

March 12—

Some people say falling sakura blossoms can be a melancholic sight, but that's how I feel when they bloom, too. I start counting how many more times I'll be alive to see them bloom. But it's not all bad. I think the flowers seem more beautiful to me than to anyone else my age. [...]

April 5—

Sophomore year, here I come! I'm in the same class as Kyōko! Yay! I'm also with Hina and Rika, and on the boys' side, Takahiro-kun. Lucky me! Well, maybe that's where all my luck with my pancreas went. Speaking of, [...]

Then, one day, she meets me.

We'd been in the same class before, but this was the day we met for real.

April 22—

For the first time, I told someone outside of my family about my illness. It's my classmate, ▆▆▆▆-kun. He just randomly found my book in the hospital and began reading it, so to hell with it! I told him. Maybe I've been wanting to tell someone. He doesn't seem to have many friends, so I think he'll keep my secret locked safely away. Actually, I've been wondering about him for a little while. We were in the same class last year, too, but I don't know if he remembers me. He's always reading his books. I get the feeling he's struggling with himself. But when I tried talking to him today, he was really funny, and I liked him right away, simple as that. ███-*kun seems a little different from other people. I'd like to get to know him better. He already knows my secret, anyway.*

She'd blacked out my name with ink. She must have gone back and done that after I told her not to put my name in her journal.

From here on, her chronology overlaps with mine. There's an entry usually every three days. Almost all of it is trivial.

April 23—

I'm a student librarian now. Writing my opinion down here won't change anything, but I'll write it anyway: What kind of school lets students switch around their activities at will?! How is this not total chaos? I tried to talk to ███-*kun today, but he looked uncomfortable. Still, it looks like he'll teach me all the library stuff anyway. I'm going to see if I can get him to talk.*

June 7—

I aced the quiz today. Classic me! I've been feeling more carefree lately. Sometimes, I joke about dying to ███-*kun, and he scrunches up his face and says something funny. I'm slowly beginning to understand the kind of person he is. He's definitely struggling with himself.*

YORU SUMINO

June 30—

It's hot. I don't hate the heat. Sweating makes me feel alive. We played basketball in gym class. ███████ *-kun asked me not to write his name in this book. I did what he'd do and said something mean, but unlike him I'm agreeable at heart, so sometimes I let him have his way. I won't write his name here anymore.*

I was right, then. When I keep reading, my name doesn't appear again. I make another connection: That's why her mother hadn't been able to identify who she'd told about her illness. When I think about the anxiety I put her family through, and I wonder if I shouldn't have made that request. The more I read, the stronger that feeling becomes.

July 8—

Someone suggested I should use my time to do the things I want. I thought about what that was, and what I came up with was… I want to do something fun with the person who told me that. I've been craving yakiniku, so we're going out to eat on Sunday. […]

July 11—

The yakiniku was so good! I had fun today. I wish I could write more about it. Too bad. All I'll say is that I'll make him see how delicious offal is before I die. After I got back, I […]

July 12—

I had to think on my feet today. After I got to school, I got the idea to go out for something sweet, so I quickly came up with a scheme to rope him in and put it into action. I spent so much time thinking about that, I probably didn't do so well on the exams.

When she stopped writing my name, she also stopped writing what she thought about me. My request had been an error.

July 13—

I'm going to start keeping a list of the things I want to do.
- *I want to go on a trip (with a boy)*
- *I want to eat tasty offal*
- *I want to eat tasty ramen*

I have an idea.

July 15—

I want to do something I'm not supposed to do with a boy who's not my boyfriend.

I'll write about the trip when I get home.

July 19—

I did better on the tests than I thought! The trip was fun, too, and Kyōko has forgiven me already, so I'm feeling good about the start of summer break... And then we get assigned summer school. Dammit.

July 21—

Today was very bad and very good. I cried a little on my own. I cried all day.

She must have been writing about *that* day—the day of our mistakes.

That she cried alone surprises me. I feel a pain near my lungs.

July 22—

I'm in the hospital. They say I have to stay here for two weeks. Some numbers were wrong or something like that. I'm a little—no, I won't lie here—I'm a lot afraid. But I'm putting up a front. Not lying to anyone. But putting up a front.

July 24—

I thought dancing might distract me from my worries, but someone came in my room and saw me. I was so embarrassed—and so relieved that he came—that I thought I was going to cry. So I hid. After that, we had a good time. I feel reassured now. [...]

July 27—

Something interesting happened, but I can't write about it. That would be against the rules. I guess I'll write about my magic tricks instead. [...]

July 28—
    I thought I had one year left. Now it's half.

I stare at the entry. I haven't been reading aloud, but I'm stunned to silence anyway.

July 31—
    I lied today. I wonder if it's the first time I've told a real lie. Someone asked me if something was going on, and I thought I was going to cry again. I almost told him. But I just couldn't. I don't want to let go of the normal life he brings to me. I'm weak. When will I tell him the truth?

August 3—
    Someone was worried for me. I told another lie. How could I be honest with him when he looked so relieved? Still, I was happy. I didn't know I could be so happy to be alive. I didn't know he needed me this badly. I was so happy, so overjoyed, I cried and cried after he left. The only reason I'm writing this now is in hopes he'll learn how I feel after I die. See, I'm weak. I think he didn't catch on, though. I've got a better poker face than you'd think.

August 4—
    I've been too wimpy lately! Enough with this depressing crap! Haven't I already decided not to write like that?! I have half a mind to go back and erase the last few days.

August 7—

Okay, so this isn't something from today, but something I've been doing during this whole stay—I've been trying to get a certain two people to run into each other as much as I can. I want them to be friends, but there's a long way to go. (Ha ha!) I hope they can start getting along before I die. I've been learning a new magic trick, and it's a big one! I can't wait to show it off. [...]

August 10—

I've decided what we're going to do when I get out of here. We're going to the ocean. I think something like that is just what we need. I think we need to slow ourselves down or we'll keep going until we've gone all the way. (Ha ha!) Not saying that would be terrible, just...not so rushed. Anyway, the magic trick is complicated. [...]

August 13—

I finally ate my first watermelon of the summer today (I know). I like watermelon better than cantaloupe. My likes haven't changed much since I was a little kid. That doesn't mean I always love offal no matter what. I hate hearing kids noisily chomping away on honeycomb tripe. I explained the rules of this book to my mom. I'll write them down just to be safe. You are absolutely not allowed to show this book to anyone outside our family until a certain person comes to take it. You're not to try to get any hints about who it is out of Kyōko, either. [...]

August 16—

    I get to leave the hospital soon! Two people came for their last visits. They both told me to quit forcing them to meet, so I scheduled them separately.

    I want the three of us to go out to eat together and get along, even if only once!

August 18—

    I leave the hospital tomorrow!!!!!!

    I'm going to enjoy every last moment I have left!

    Yeah!!!!!!!!!!!!

Her journal cuts short there.

I can't believe it. I *had* been right to be afraid.

Something had been going on, and she had hidden it.

I feel something building up inside my guts. *Steady,* I tell myself, doing all I can to keep it together. *You couldn't have done anything about it then, and you can't do anything about it now.*

Breathing deeply, I direct my thoughts toward the present.

I didn't find what I was seeking in her book. Its pages contain no clear answer to my biggest question: What was I to her? I can see I was important to her; I knew that already. But what did she call me in her thoughts?

I'm despondent.

I close my eyes and ease my breathing. Unintentionally, I turn this moment into one of silence, almost prayer-like.

I close the book and notice her mother is quietly waiting for me. I softly rest the book on the tatami mat and slide it toward her.

"Thank you," I say.

"There's more."

The silence returns. Then I say, "What?"

She doesn't take the book. Her eyes, just like her daughter's, except reddened by crying, are locked on mine as she says, "What Sakura really wanted you to read comes after that."

I quickly scoop up the book and flip through the blank pages. Near the end of the book, her writing starts up again.

Her handwriting looks buoyant and lively and reminds me of who she was.

My breath stops.

Farewell Letters [rough draft] [of many]

———

To whom it may concern, (all of you)

This is my goodbye.

If you are reading this right now, then I must be dead. (Is that too cliché?)

I want to begin by apologizing for hiding my illness from nearly everyone. I'm truly sorry.

Keeping this secret has been selfish of me, but I wanted to keep living a normal life, where we could all share in fun times and laughter. And now I've died without telling you.

Some of you may have some things you wish you could have told me. If that's true for you, then go to everyone who isn't me and tell them the things you wish for them to know. I want you to tell them if you love them, if you hate them, and everything. They could die at any time, just like me. It's too late to tell me now, but you can still tell them. I hope you will.

———

To everyone at school, [maybe pick out a few to address directly?]

I had so much fun studying with all of you. The cultural festival and sports day were really fun, but what most made me happy were the average days where I could just be with everyone. I'm sad I won't be able to see where you all go and what you end up doing. Make all the memories you can and tell them to me in heaven. So no bad behavior allowed! (Ha ha!) To everyone who liked me, and everyone who didn't, thank you.

———

Mom, Dad, big brother, [probably should write separate messages here at least?]

Thank you for everything. I love having you as my family. I really, and truly love each of you. When I was still little, we used to go on trips, the four of us. I still remember them well. I know I was a handful, to put it lightly, but I hope I grew into a daughter you could be proud of.

Whatever comes next, if there's a heaven, or reincarnation, or anything else, I want to be your daughter again. So, you two need to keep loving each other. When you're reborn, I want you both to raise me again. I want to be a Yamauchi again, with my parents and my brother. Hrm. There's too much I want to write. I have to figure out what to keep.

———

[Okay I definitely need to write separate messages to everyone who's important to me. I'll rewrite the family section later.]

———

Kyōko.

I'm going to start by saying I love you.

I love you Kyōko. There's no mistaking it. I love you. And so, I'm sorry.

I'm sorry I didn't tell you until the very end. [Maybe I shouldn't wait. Think about when to tell her.]

I can't ask you to forgive me.

But please, just believe this: I loved you.

That's why I couldn't tell you.

I loved being with you. Laughing, ranting, being silly, crying... I loved all of it.

No, not loved—love.

Forever. Not past tense, but present and continuous. Whether I'm in heaven or if I'm reborn, I'll always love you.

I don't have the courage or the strength to destroy the time I get to spend with you.

To all my other friends, I'm sorry, but Kyōko will always be number one. Who knows, maybe I'm even in love with Kyōko. That settles it, in your next life, Kyōko, you should be born as a boy. (Ha ha!)

Be happy, Kyōko.

I know that whatever happens to you, you'll be fine. Nothing can beat you.

Find a perfect husband, have adorable babies, and build a family happier than any other.

I really wish I could see your future *family* [← Don't cry when you write this for real.]

I'll always be watching over you from heaven.

Oh, one last thing. I want you to do one thing for me. Think of it as my last request.

There's someone I want you to start getting along with.

You know who it is. Yes, the boy you're always glaring at.

He's a good person. He really is. Even if he teases me sometimes.

But he is

[I can finish writing about him later, ha]

[Write your feelings to Kyōko better.]

————

Finally, to you.

Don't worry, I won't write your name.

You. You. You, who told me not to write your name.

So, what's up?

Lately—and I'm writing this summer of sophomore year—I've had a lot more I want to tell you.

Let's deal with the business stuff first.

This book is now yours, freely.

I've told my family as much. When you come to take it, they're to give it to you.

By freely, I mean you can do whatever you want with this book.

Destroy it, hide it, give it away, whatever.

As you've probably already seen, I've written letters to other people in these pages, but it's up to you whether or not you show them.

The moment you're reading this, <u>Living with Dying</u> is now your possession. If you don't want it, you can throw it away. (Grrrr)

I wish I had a better way to thank you for everything you've given me, but it's the best I can do.

That watermelon you brought the other day was really good. [Why am I writing about something that just happened? I guess I can just rewrite this part later.]

Okay. I'm going to write down everything I want to tell you right now. These are my true feelings, as far as I understand them. If anything changes, I'll rewrite this part. Although if I start hating you I won't write about it. If that happens, I can just have Kyōko kill you, and I won't need to bother. (Ha ha!)

It's only been four months since we met in the hospital.

*That's so weird. I feel like I've spent a much, much longer
time with you. I'm sure the time seems fuller because of all
the things you've taught me.*

*I already mentioned this in my journal, but the truth
is I'd been curious about you for a long time. Do you know
why? I've heard you say it often.*

The answer: You and I are opposite people.

I've thought so myself.

*I'd been wanting to learn more about you, but I never
had an opportunity to get closer to you. And then you
happened to pick up my book. I thought, well, now we'll
just have to get along. And we did. I'm glad we did.*

*Recently, I've been wondering every now and then if·
maybe we've been getting along a little too well.*

*This thing we're doing—sometimes I think of it as
playing at being in love—it makes my heart race. So far, all
we're doing is hugging, which is fine. But I wonder, at this
rate, if we'll soon be kissing as part of our game. And there
goes my heart racing again.*

*Well, I guess I wouldn't object. Does that shock you?
I really mean it. As long as it was still make believe, I'd
be fine.*

*I wasn't sure if I'd admit this to you, but, well, if
you're reading this, then I'm dead, so why not? I'll be open
with you.*

*So here goes. I don't know how many times I've
thought that I'm in love with you. Once was when you told*

me about your first crush. I felt a knot in my chest. When we were drinking in our hotel room was another. The first time I hugged you.

But I didn't want to cross that line and become boyfriend and girlfriend. And I won't ever want that. I think. Probably.

Maybe we could have worked out together, romantically. But we don't have enough time to find out, do we?

I also don't want to define our relationship with common words like those.

Love? Friendship? That's not what we have, is it? If you were in love with me, maybe that would be different. I kind of wonder sometimes. But I wouldn't know how to ask, even if I wanted to.

Oh, and since this has to do with the game of truth or dare I asked you to play in the hospital, I'll tell you what I was trying to ask you. Since I can't find out what your answer is, this won't break any rules.

What I wanted to ask you was...

Why don't you ever say my name?

Do you remember how you woke me on the bullet train? I do. You smacked me with a rubber band. You could have woken me by saying my name, but you didn't. I've wondered about that ever since. I began noticing you never called me by my name. Not even once. It's always "you." You, you, you.

When I asked you to play that one round, I had been considering asking you. But part of me was afraid it was because you didn't like me. That's how I think sometimes. And if that had been your answer, I couldn't have just shrugged it off. I'm not confident enough to not care. Unlike you, I can't build myself as a person without relying on the people around me.

If I was ever going to ask you, I needed a push—the game of truth or dare.

But now I think there's a different reason you never say my name.

What I'm about to say is just a guess. Forgive me if I'm wrong.

Are you scared of defining who I am to you?

You told me that when people say your name, you like to speculate what you are to them. And you don't care if you're right or not, because it's in your head.

Now, maybe this is just what I want to believe, but I think you do care about me.

And that's why you're afraid to speculate what I am to you.

You don't want to say my name, because you might attach a meaning to it.

You're afraid to define someone you're going to lose as a "friend" or "girlfriend."

Well? How about it? If I'm right, I'll accept an offering of plum liquor by my grave.

You don't have to be afraid. No matter what happens, there should always be a way to get along with people. Just like you and me.

I keep saying you're afraid of this or that, so maybe it sounds like I'm calling you a coward, but I'm not.

I think you're an amazing person.

You're an amazing person who is exactly my opposite.

While I'm at it, I'll answer your question, too. What a lucky day for you!

You know which question I mean, right? You asked me what I think of you. Or maybe you don't care. You can skip this part if you want.

I...

I wish I could be like you.

I've been thinking that for a little while now.

If I was like you, maybe I could take responsibility for my life and find what makes me uniquely special, just for myself, without inflicting sadness on you or my family, and without being such a burden on others.

Don't get me wrong, I'm truly happy with my life as it is right now. But I admire you for being able to live as your own person, whether anyone else is around you or not.

My life is based upon someone always being there with me.

At one point, I realized something.

Without anyone around me, I am nothing special.

I don't think that's a bad thing. I mean, everyone's

like that, right? People are who they are through their relationships with others. Take our classmates—without their friends and boyfriends and girlfriends, who would they be?

Being compared to others, comparing ourselves to others—that's how we discover who we are.

That's what living means to me.

But you, and you alone, are always on your own.

You found what makes yourself special outside of any social connections, by looking only at yourself.

I want to be able to do that for myself.

That's why, after you went home that day, I cried.

That day, you genuinely worried for me. That day, you told me you wanted me to live.

You had decided you didn't need any friend or anyone to love. But then you chose to need someone.

And not just someone. You chose me.

For the first time, I realized someone needed me for who I was.

For the first time, I realized I was unique.

Thank you.

I might have been waiting seventeen years for you to need me.

Like a sakura flower waiting for spring.

Maybe some part of me recognized that, so I chose to record my thoughts in this book, even though I hardly ever read books.

I made a choice, and I met you.

You really are incredible, you know that? To be able to make someone as happy as you make me. I wish everyone could see your charm.

I noticed it a long time ago.

What's that old saying? Before I die, I want to make a potion from the dirt under your nails.

Now that I write that out, that seems too plain to describe us. Our connection is wasted on some cliché like that.

I think you know what I'm going to say.

Like it or not.

I want to eat your pancreas.

(I wrote the longest about you. I bet Kyōko will be mad about that, so I better fix that later.)

The end. [of the first draft]

I finish reading and return to a world in which she's gone.

And I notice something...

I'm breaking.

I'm aware it's happening, but I'm powerless to stop it.

Before I fall apart, there's one thing I must know.

I say, "Do you have her—Sakura-san's cell phone?"

"Her phone?"

Her mother stands and walks out of the room. Soon, she

returns with a flip phone and says, "When she...left us, we kept her phone around, so we could answer it, but we've been keeping it turned off now."

"Please, I want to see it."

Without another word, her mother hands me the phone.

I flip the cell open and turn it on. After a moment, I open her incoming text folder.

There, among countless unopened messages, I find it.

The last message I sent to her.

The message had been opened.

She saw it.

I place her phone and her book on the tatami mat. I somehow manage to work my shaking lips to say one last thing before I break.

"Mrs...Yamauchi?"

"Yes?"

"I'm sorry, I know, this isn't my place... But..."

She allows me to finish.

"Can I cry now?"

A tear rolls down her cheek, and she nods once.

I break down. But no, the truth is, I broke a long time ago.

I cry. I cry like a baby, feeling no shame, with heaving sobs. I press my cheek against the tatami; I face the ceiling; I wail. I've never cried like this before or cried at all in front of another person. I never wanted to. I didn't want to push my own sadness onto someone else. So I never have. But too many emotions surge through me to contain them any longer.

I'm happy.

My message reached her.

She needed me.

I was able to help her.

I'm happy.

But I'm in more pain than I ever imagined possible.

Her voice echoes in my mind.

Her face appears, wearing one expression after another.

She's crying, she's angry, she's smiling, and smiling, and smiling.

Her touch.

Her smell.

That sweet fragrance.

I remember every aspect of her as if they are still here—as if she is still here.

But she's not. She's not here.

She's not anywhere. My eyes were always on her but can't find her now.

She liked to say our outlooks didn't match up.

Of course they didn't.

We were never looking in the same direction.

We were always looking at each other.

Standing at the edge of the water, looking to the opposite shore.

We never would have known we were looking at each other. We never would have noticed. We occupied separate places, with nothing to connect us.

But then she leapt across the gulf, and we met.

And yet I still thought I was the only one who needed the other—who wanted to become like the other.

I never thought anyone would want to be like me.

But she did.

And now I find a new belief.

I was born to meet her.

All the choices I've made in life were for one purpose: to meet her.

I have no doubts.

I know it must be true, because nothing has ever brought me this much joy or this much pain.

I'm alive.

Because of her, for the past four months, I've truly lived.

For the first time, I'm alive.

Because we shared a connection.

Thank you, thank you, thank you.

Words could never express the depths of my gratitude, and she isn't here to hear them.

No matter how hard I cry, my tears won't reach her anymore.

No matter how loud I shout, my voice won't reach her anymore.

I so badly wish I could tell her—

My joy and my pain.

That I had more fun with her than any other time in my life.

That I wanted more time with her.

That I wanted us to be together always.

I know it's impossible, but I wish I could tell her, even if it served no purpose other than to make myself feel better.

My heart aches.

I won't be able to tell her anything anymore.

I won't be able to do anything to help her anymore.

Even after she gave me so much.

I can do nothing.

Nine

I CRY. I CRY AND I CRY.

And then—

I stop crying. Not by choice, but as a function of my physiology. I lift my head and see her mother still with me, waiting.

She hands me a blue handkerchief. Hesitantly, I accept the cloth and dry my tears as I catch my breath.

She says, "You can keep it. It's Sakura's. She'd be happy for you to have it."

"Thank you."

I finish drying my eyes, nose, and mouth before putting the handkerchief in my pocket.

I shift position on the tatami mat and sit up straight. My eyes are red now, too.

"I'm sorry for breaking down like that," I say.

Immediately, she shakes her head and says, "No, it's fine. Children should be allowed to cry. She cried a lot, too. She was always something of a crybaby. But after she met you, and you started spending time together, like she wrote in her journal, she stopped crying. Not completely, of course, but a lot less. Thank you. The time you gave her was precious."

I have to hold back the tears for a moment to make sure I don't start crying again. Then I shake my head and say, "She gave me something precious."

"I wish we could have all shared a meal together, as a family. She never said anything about you to us."

She smiles at me sadly and I waver again.

I let myself waver as I begin talking a little about my memories of her. I tell her mother about things that weren't in the journal—leaving out the game of truth or dare and how we shared a bed. She nods along as she listens.

As I speak, the weight of my emotions slowly begins to lift. The important joys and sorrows remain, but the parts I don't need to hold onto seem to fall away.

I begin thinking the mother is listening to me for my sake.

When I'm ready to stop, I ask one more favor.

"Can I come back to visit again?"

"Of course. I'd like for you to meet the rest of our family. You could bring Kyōko-chan, but... Ah, but from the sound of things, you're not on very friendly terms."

She laughs softly, just like her daughter.

"Yeah, you could say that. The way things happened, she hates me."

"Someday, if that ever changes, I hope you both can come

over for dinner together. Partly because I want to thank you, but seeing the two people she most cared about getting along would make me happy as her mother."

I say, "That's more up to Kyōko-san than me, but I'll take it to heart."

After we exchange a few more words, I promise to come back another day, then stand up. She strongly insists I take *Living with Dying*, and I do. She refuses the 10,000-yen my mother had me bring.

She walks me to the front door. I put on my shoes, thank her again, and have my hand on the doorknob when she says, casually, "You told me your family name, but not your given name. What is it?"

I look over my shoulder and answer, "It's Haruki. Shiga Haruki."

"Oh," she says. "Isn't there a novelist with that name?"

I'm taken by surprise, and I feel a smile come to my lips. "Yeah. Although I don't know which one you mean."

I thank her one last time, say goodbye, and leave the Yamauchi's house.

The rain has stopped.

When I get home, my mother is already there. She sees my face and says, "Good man." My dad comes home during dinner, and he slaps me on the back. I guess I should stop underestimating them.

After the meal, I close myself back in my room and read *Living with Dying* again. As I turn the pages, I think about what

I should do from here. I end up stopping to cry three times, but I still think. What can I do for her, for her family, and for me?

Now that I have her book, what can I do?

Sometime after nine o'clock, I make a decision and act on it.

I retrieve a printout from my desk drawer and flip open my cell phone.

Looking at the paper, I dial a number I thought I'd go my whole life never dialing.

When I go to sleep, I dream I'm talking with the girl, and I cry again.

I arrive at the café after noon.

I'm a little early, and the person I'm supposed to meet isn't here yet. I order an iced coffee and sit in an open seat by the window.

I didn't choose the meeting place, but I knew the way here. By chance, this is the same café where I waited for the girl on the day she died.

Or maybe this isn't chance, I think as I drink my coffee. The pair probably went here often.

Just as on that day, I gaze out the window. Just as on that day, all kinds of people pass by, living all kinds of lives.

Unlike that day, the person I'm supposed to meet shows up right on time. Ah, good. Her arrival comes as a relief. Not just because of residual trauma; I also thought I may get stood up.

Without a word, Kyōko-san sits down across from me at the table and immediately turns her puffy, red-eyed glare at me.

"Well, I'm here," she says reluctantly. "What do you want?"

I don't falter. I force my nerves down and respond to her glare by opening my mouth. But before I can say anything, she interrupts me.

"You... You didn't come to Sakura's funeral."

I don't say anything.

"Why didn't you?"

"I..."

I'm searching to find an answer and failing when she slaps her hands on the table. The noise resounds through the café, and for a second, time seems to stop.

When time resumes, I avert my eyes and say in a small voice, "Sorry."

I clear my throat and begin speaking again. "Thank you for coming. I guess this is the first time we're having a real talk."

She doesn't say anything.

I continue, "You're here because I told you I needed to speak with you, but where should I start?"

"Just get to the point."

"Yes, right. Sorry. I have something to show you."

More silence.

What I want to talk about is, and could only be, the girl. She's the only connection between Kyōko-san and myself. I took almost all of last evening deciding to do this.

Up until the moment I arrived at the café, I'd been considering how to approach this conversation. Should I start with my relationship with her? Should I start with her sickness? In the end, I decided to start by showing her best friend the truth.

I take *Living with Dying* from my school bag and place the book on the table.

Confused, Kyōko-san says, "A book?"

"It's titled *Living with Dying*."

"'Living...with dying'?"

I remove the plain book protector and show her the cover.

Kyōko-san's somewhat hollow eyes open wide with recognition. I'm both impressed and jealous.

She says, "That's... That's Sakura's handwriting."

I nod sharply. "This is her book. She wrote it for other people to read after her death, and she gave it to me."

"What do you mean, after her death?"

I feel a weight on my chest. This won't be easy to say. But I can't stop now.

"Everything she wrote inside this book," I explain, "is all true. This isn't one of her pranks, and it's not one of mine. She mostly used the book like a diary, but in the back, she wrote goodbyes. One is for you. Another is for me, too."

"What are you saying?"

"She was sick."

"You're lying. I would have known."

"She didn't tell you."

"Why would she tell you, but not me?"

I had the same question once, but now I know the answer.

I say, "I was the only person she told. She died a different way, but if that hadn't happened to her, then—"

I'm interrupted. My ears ring, and pain blossoms in my left cheek. I've never been slapped before, so it takes me a while to realize what happened.

Kyōko-san's eyes water, and she pleads, "Stop."

"I will not. I have to tell you this, Kyōko-san. She wrote in this book that you're the most important person to her. That's why I want you to listen now. She was sick. If she hadn't been killed, she would have died within six months. I'm telling you the truth."

Kyōko-san weakly shakes her head.

I slide the book toward her. "Read it," I say. "She liked pranking people, but you know she would never hurt you as a joke."

I decide not to say more.

I'm a little worried she won't read the book, but after a little while, Kyōko-san reaches out her hand and dispels my concern.

Hesitantly, she takes the book and opens its pages.

"It's really her handwriting," she says.

"I swear to you, it's genuine."

Eyebrows furrowed, Kyōko-san begins slowly reading the first page. I focus on waiting for her.

The girl told me once, before she died, that her friend didn't read very often. Kyōko-san would need time to read. Of course, her reading speed alone won't be the only reason she might take a long time.

At first, Kyōko-san seems to have trouble believing her eyes, as she reads and re-reads the same pages several times. Sometimes,

I think I see her mouthing, *It's not true.* Then a connection is made, her reading pace slows, and like a switch has flipped, she begins crying.

I don't feel the slightest impatience when Kyōko-san starts to cry—just relief. If she had refused to believe the book, this meeting would have been for nothing. The girl's goodbye wouldn't have reached her, and my other goal would have failed.

While Kyōko-san reads, I finish two cups of coffee. I order her an orange juice, and she drinks from the glass without a word.

As I wait, I don't think of the girl. Instead, I think about what I can do with what she gave me. Since I'm only used to thinking about myself in isolation, it doesn't come easy, and time passes quickly as I try.

At some point, I notice the daylight has begun to fade. I haven't found any more concrete answers than I had the night before. Things that come naturally to other people are difficult for me.

Kyōko-san's face is a teary mess, and a pile of damp tissues sits on the table. She is about halfway through the book when she starts to close it. I do the same thing as the girl's mother did yesterday.

"There's more," I say.

Kyōko-san already looks tired from crying, but she reads through the end before closing the book, this time for real. She begins weeping, loudly, oblivious to the people around us, and I stay with her, as the mother did for me. Kyōko-san calls out her friend's name, *Sakura, Sakura,* over and over.

She cries even longer than I did the day before, and before she's stopped, she looks up at me, her eyes every bit as hostile as before.

"Why?" she says with a raspy voice. "Why keep it from me?"

"It's like she said, she—"

"Not her. You! Why didn't *you* tell me?"

Taken aback by her anger, I can't find any response. Any words I might possibly say wither away beneath her messy, yet deadly-sharp glare.

"If you'd told me... If you'd only said something, I could have had more time with her. I would have quit volleyball. I would have quit school! I could have been with her..."

Now I understand the source of her anger.

"I'll never forgive you," she says. "I don't care how important you were to her, or how much she needed you, or even if she loved you. I'll never forgive you."

She hides her face again and her tears begin falling to the floor. In this moment, a tiny part of me is ready to accept her hating me, just as I would have before. She can hate me, I don't mind. But I shake my head. No. That's not who I need to be.

I resolve myself to speak, even as her head hangs low.

"I'm sorry," I say. "But I would like you to forgive me, even if it takes a long time."

Kyōko-san says nothing.

I push aside my nervousness and somehow continue.

"And...if it's all right with you...I..."

She isn't looking at me.

My throat tightens, and my heart seems to stop as I say something I've never said to anyone before.

"I would like to be your friend."

I try steadying my breath. The effort takes all of my focus, leaving me no way to gauge her reaction.

She's still silent.

"I'm not asking because she wanted me to. This is my choice. I want us to get along. I want to get along with you."

Nothing.

"Or is that...just not possible?"

I don't know how else to ask. So now, I stay quiet. Silence falls between us.

I've never felt so nervous waiting for another person's answer. All my thoughts remain on myself, selfishly so, as I wait for her to respond. Eventually, still looking down, she shakes her head several times, stands, and leaves without looking at me.

As I watch her leave, it's my turn to hang my head.

I failed.

My bill has come due, I realize. I've spent my entire life never trying to interact with other people, and this is the cost.

I mutter to myself, "This is hard."

Or maybe not to myself—to the girl.

I pick up the book from the table, put it back in my bag, and clean up the accumulated trash before stepping outside into the darkness.

What should I do next? I feel as if I'm trapped in a maze with no exit. From the maze, I can look up and see the sky. I can see there's an outside, but I can't get there.

What a tangled problem. How amazing that other people can navigate and solve these kinds of issues on a daily basis.

I ride my bicycle back home.

Summer vacation is almost over.

This is one assignment I know I won't be finishing before school starts again.

Ten

WITH THE END OF SUMMER SCHOOL yesterday, my summer vacation truly begins today. Spurred onward by the cicadas ceaselessly droning at my backside, I climb the stone steps.

The day is exceptionally hot, with the sun blazing, its light assaulting me from above and reflecting off the rocks to attack from below. My T-shirt is already drenched.

No, I'm not punishing myself out of some self-inflicted penance.

A girl walking ahead looks over her shoulder at me and grins. I'm drenched in sweat and out of breath.

She says, "Do you always gotta be such a wuss?"

The remark annoys me, and I consider making a rebuttal, but I decide to wait until I have my breath back. For now, I focus on getting up these stairs as quickly as I can.

Having no trouble herself, she claps twice and says, "C'mon, you can do it." From her expression, I can't tell if she's cheering me on or taunting me.

When we finally reach the top, I wipe myself down with a towel and mount my defense.

"I'm different from you," I say.

"Yeah, you're a guy. If you can't keep up with me, that's sad."

"Look, we of noble birth have no need to exert ourselves."

"I'm sure the nobles can do just fine."

I take a plastic tea bottle from my backpack and gulp the liquid down. The girl keeps briskly walking ahead. I follow her, and after a little while the hillside trees fall away to reveal a beautiful view over our city.

She spreads her arms and says, "This feels great!"

Between the view and the wind, it does feel great. As the breeze dries my sweat, I take another drink of tea to fortify myself.

I say, "Let's go. We're almost there."

"That's the spirit! Here, I'll reward you with some candy."

"Do you two think I exist solely on candy and gum?"

I'm reminded of my other friend, the guy who keeps offering me gum in school.

She says, "I can't help it if I happen to carry some candy in my pocket. Just take it."

Grumbling, I accept the candy and put it in my pocket, where it joins several of its companions.

She hums a tune as she walks with lively steps, and I trudge along behind her, until I suddenly feel conscious of our imbalance of strength. I force my head high and my shoulders back.

Square stones replace the dirt path, and we arrive at our destination. Among the rows of stone monuments, we find the one we seek.

She says, "Okay, you're on water duty, Haruki. Go bring us some, would you?"

"Two points. First, what duty are you on, and second, why don't we just go together?"

"Quit whining. I gave you candy, didn't I?"

I can't believe her nerve, but I also know any further protests will be useless. I quietly set down my things and walk to a nearby water spigot, where wooden buckets and ladles are ready. I take one of each and fill the bucket from the tap. When I return to the girl's side, she's looking up at the sky.

"Thanks," she says, adding archly, "That must have been hard."

"If you think so, then you should have helped."

"I would have, but you see, I'm of noble birth, so..."

"Yeah, yeah. Here you go, m'lady."

I hand her the bucket and ladle. She respectfully takes them and roughly flings the purifying waters onto the Yamauchi's family grave. Droplets splash off the stone and splatter on my cheek. The gravestone, shiny with water, reflects the sunlight and takes on a sacred quality.

She shouts, "Hey, Sakura, wake up!"

"I'm pretty sure that's not how you're supposed to do...any of that."

Not paying any attention to what I said, she continues splashing the water onto the gravestone until the last drop is gone. She looks like she's feeling good, working up a sweat, and for a moment, I wonder if this is some sort of sport I'd never heard of.

She asks, "When you put your hands together in front of a grave, are you supposed to, like, clap?"

"Normally, no. But for her, I think we should."

We stand in front of her grave and clap our hands once. Getting along together, we close our eyes and pray for her to hear our thoughts.

After a long prayer, we open our eyes at almost the same time and place our offerings.

She asks, "Should we go to her house now?"

"Yeah," I say.

"Fair warning—her mother and I are going to lecture the crap out of you today."

"What?" I say incredulously. "I can't think of a single reason why."

"There's so many reasons, I hardly know where to start." She holds up a finger. "Oh, how about how it's summer of your senior year and you're just coasting, too cocky to study at all."

"Hey, I'm smart, I don't need to study."

"That's what I'm talking about!"

Her wisecrack disappears into the blue summer sky, while my thoughts are on the last time I went to the Yamauchi's house. The last time I was there, I met her older brother, and he shared stories with me.

Returning from my memories, I say, "This will be my first time going over there with someone else."

"Yeah, you're going to be hearing about that, too."

We exchange a pointless but fun back-and-forth, and this time, we return the bucket and ladle together. We return to the gravesite, and I announce, "We're going over to your house," and start back the way we came. I'm not thrilled by the idea of walking that path again, but all that's left to do here is exchange a pointless but fun back-and-forth, and that just wouldn't be productive.

On the way back, as on the way here, I follow after Kyōko-san.

I put my hands together and close my eyes.

My thoughts are my own, and I send them to you.

Forgive me for my thoughts now. For my prayers.

I'm going to start with a complaint, because that's what I do.

This hasn't been easy. This isn't as easy as you said; as it was for you.

Interacting with other people isn't easy.

It's hard. It really is.

That's why this has taken me a year, although I admit I'm partly to blame.

But I made my choices, and I've come this far now. I hope that you'll approve.

One year ago, I made a choice to become a person like you—a person who could get to know others; someone capable of love.

I don't know if I'm there yet, but at least I made that choice.

After this, I'm going to your house together with your best friend—my first friend.

I wish it was the three of us going, but that's not possible now. I'll just do what I can. We'll have to save that get-together for heaven.

If you're wondering why your best friend and I are going to your house when you're not there, I'm fulfilling a promise I made to your mother almost a year ago.

What took me so long, you ask? That's what Kyōko-san said to me, too.

I have an excuse. The life I've led left me unequipped with the knowledge of certain things, like at what point you can call someone your friend.

And I believed taking Kyōko-san to your house wouldn't count until we had become friends.

The only other relationship I could measure against was the one you and I shared.

After Kyōko-san told me she would never forgive me, we walked the path toward friendship one step at a time. The path was new to me, and even though she's not a patient person, she patiently waited for me despite my faltering footsteps. I'm deeply thankful for her. She's my best friend, although of course I'd never tell her that.

That's where things stood when I took her to the place you and I went a year ago—although Kyōko-san and I didn't stay overnight. That's when I told her about the promise I made to your mother, and she got mad at me for not telling her sooner.

My friend does have a temper.

I'm leaving you a present I bought on that trip.

You'll recognize it—it's made from plums near the god of education's home.

You're still only eighteen, but I'll look the other way. I tried a little—just a taste test—and it's good stuff.

I hope you like it.

Kyōko-san is doing well. I guess you probably know that.

I am, too. So much better than before I met you.

After you died, I thought I'd been born to meet you.

But I didn't believe your life's purpose was to be needed by me.

Now, I think about us differently.

I believe our lives brought us to be together.

We weren't enough on our own.

Our purpose was to provide what the other was missing.

At least, that's how I've been thinking lately.

And now that you're gone, I need to learn how to stand on my own.

That's what I can do to honor the complete person we became together.

I'll come back to visit you again. I don't know what happens to people's souls when they die, so I'll repeat all this to your photograph in your house. If you don't hear me either time, I'll tell you in heaven.

Bye for now.

...

Oh, one more thing. I almost forgot. There's something I never admitted to you.

I told you a lie.

In your book, you admitted how you cried, what you felt about me, and the lies you told. In the interest of fairness, I've decided I'd admit something to you.

Are you ready?

Do you remember how I told you about my first crush? That was a lie.

The girl who added "-san" to everything? I made her up.

I was going to tell you, but you seemed so moved by my story, I couldn't do it.

Maybe I'll tell you the real answer the next time we meet.

And if another girl like my true first crush comes into my life again...

Maybe that time, I'll eat her pancreas.

We descend the staircase, its white stone steps glittering under the harsh light of the relentless sun.

Ahead of me, Kyōko-san hums a song as her gym bag swings from her shoulder.

I catch up to my happy friend. Walking beside her, I name the song.

She looks embarrassed and thwaps me on the shoulder.

I laugh, then I look to the sky and say a thought just as it enters my mind.

"Let's be happy."

"Is that your way of confessing your love for me? On the way back from Sakura's *grave*? Tacky."

"Certainly not. I'm talking about in a bigger sense." I grin. Taunting the girl who forgave me when others never could have,

I add, "Besides, unlike some other guy, I'm into the quieter types."

I immediately realize my mistake. But immediately is too late, and Kyōko-san tilts her head with suspicion. I swear I can see the question mark appear above her.

"Unlike what other guy?"

"Um, nope. Never mind that. I didn't say anything."

She watches me as I go through the rare experience of being flustered, and she thinks for a moment. Then the edges of her lips curl up, and she claps her hands. The clap makes a pleasant echo off the rocks, even if her smile is anything but.

I shake my head and plead, "Listen, I really didn't mean to say that, so if you could just not tell him…"

"If you had more friends, I might not have known who it was. But really, him? Huh. I thought *he* was more into the quiet types."

I thought so, too. After all, he'd told me so himself. I don't know if his tastes changed, or if he'd been lying in the first place. It doesn't really matter which, but for now I send him my sincere apologies. Sorry; next time, I'll give you the gum.

Meanwhile, Kyōko-san is still smirking and muttering the occasional, "Huh," and "Hmmm."

I ask, "Are you glad?"

"Well, you know, it doesn't feel bad to be liked by someone."

"That's good," I say, for everyone involved, including my blundering self.

She adds, "But I don't think I want to start dating anyone until after the college entrance exams."

"Planning ahead, huh? I'll let him know. Maybe that way he'll want to study."

We playfully needle each other as we walk down the stairs.

Suddenly, I hear laughter coming from behind. I turn my head so fast it nearly unscrews from my neck. Kyōko-san does the same. Wincing in pain, she brings her hand to her neck.

No one is behind us, of course.

Wind caresses my sweat-streaked face.

Kyōko-san and I turn to each other. Our eyes meet, and we laugh.

She says, "We'd better go to Sakura's house."

"Yeah, she'll be waiting for us."

We laugh again and continue down the long stairs.

I'm not afraid anymore.